VITAL ORGANS

A STORY OF MEDICINE, MONEY, AND MURDER IN THE NAME OF SCIENCE

Allan Zelinger

ISBN: 1495405648
ISBN 13: 9781495405648

1

Ramon peered through a window of the white building. It was noon and the sun blazed overhead. He watched as a lizard scurried into shade then shifted the toothpick in his mouth.

From the back of the room Hector called out, "Hey, *compadre,* come give me a hand." Ramon walked over and helped Hector lift the corpse onto a wooden table. Emptied of its internal organs, the body weighed less than normal.

Hector, a hulk of a man, raised his machete then brought it down hard. The sound of snapping bone reverberated through the room as an arm fell off.

Ramon plopped down on a sofa to watch the soccer game on television, while Hector continued his chopping. When he was done, the body parts were distributed into three large plastic bags.

They carried the bags to a car parked outside and tossed them inside the trunk. Ramon cleared his throat and addressed his deceased colleague with an impromptu eulogy.

"Manulo, we had some good times together but you should have known better than to steal from the patron. Please forgive us but it's your own fucking fault that you're dead."

Finished with the speech, Ramon and Hector made a sign of the cross, then Ramon slammed the lid shut.

No sooner had they driven out the front gate than Hector began maneuvering his massive body around to reach for a cooler on the back seat. It was stocked with Corona beer and ham sandwiches he prepared before embarking.

"You want something to eat?" he politely asked Ramon.

The driver shot back, "How the fuck can you eat right after hacking someone to pieces?"

Ramon couldn't remember a time when Hector wasn't hungry. No matter how gruesome the job, nothing seemed to blunt the big man's appetite.

Finishing his snack, Hector licked his fingers clean and wiped them on his shirt. Suddenly, the car veered off the road and drove into the desert. Ramon did his best to avoid rocks and cacti, but the route was rough. At one point the car lurched upward and came down hard. They heard jostling inside the truck.

"Say, take it easy," Hector implored. "You don't want Manulo to complain about the ride, do you?"

Both of them laughed, while Ramon continued driving down the bumpy path.

2

A red Porsche sped down the highway and turned off onto an unmarked road. Up ahead a structure took shape from the desert landscape. The top of the adobe wall surrounding the compound glistened like diamonds as the sunlight played off the razor wire. When the car was close, a guard with an AK-47 waved the driver through the front gate.

The Porsche halted in front of a white building, the largest structure at the site. A moment later its door popped open, and Dr. Ricky Pedraza stepped out.

Before leaving home, Ricky had been lying by his swimming pool, reading a magazine and sipping a cup of coffee. The villa where he lived was situated on a bluff overlooking the Pacific on the northern outskirts of Mazatlan. From there he had a magnificent view of the bay, which centuries before hid pirates preying on treasure-laden Spanish galleons. Now the beach was lined with resort hotels, and luxury cruise liners lay anchored offshore. The sunshine and white sand made the location a tourist paradise and earned the city its nickname, "Pearl of the Pacific."

Christina, his girlfriend, was lying topless on a lounger next to his. She was a stunning beauty with long legs, sparkling green eyes, and flowing jet-black hair.

She picked up a purse at her side, pulled out a vial, and then asked, "You want some, Ricky?"

He turned to look then shook his head no while she made a line of cocaine and inhaled. Ricky used the drug only sparingly and almost never recreationally. When he had to perform surgery all day and continue through the night, that's when a little cocaine came in handy.

Pedraza had hooked up with Christina several months before, meeting her at a nightclub in the city. Afterward they drove to the private marina where he harbored his boat. Powered by twin twelve-hundred horsepower engines, it could hit one hundred miles per hour at full throttle. The hull was yellow with red racing stripes. On its stern in bold letters was the name, *El Scalpel.*

On board they drank champagne. Before long both were naked, and Ricky sat in the captain's seat while Christina mounted him. Their voracious lovemaking rocked the boat, sending wavelets into the harbor's still water.

Christina moved from her lounger onto Ricky's and began massaging suntan oil onto his chest, as Ricky tried to maintain concentration on his magazine.

"Hey, I'm trying to read," he protested, pushing her hand away.

"Come on, Ricky, be nice."

Christina leaned forward and kissed him with moist, inviting lips. He felt her breasts pressing against his skin. Christina's fingertips journeyed under the front of his swimsuit, and she began to touch him enticingly. He didn't need more coaxing. Flipping the magazine onto the ground, he pulled her on top of him.

Ricky's hand traveled down to her bikini bottom. He reached between her legs and felt her rhythmically pressing against him inviting his entry. Suddenly, his cellphone rang, and the lovemaking halted.

"Ricky, I hate like hell to bother you," the man on the line said with a Texas drawl, "but we've got a case out at the white building." He went on. "I'm on my way there now, and I'll need you as soon as possible."

Ricky responded angrily, "What? You can't be serious. It's my fucking day off!"

"Believe me, I wish I didn't have to ask you, but I can't find Jamison anywhere."

For a moment there was silence on the line, then he relented. "All right, I'll come but get the case started as soon as you arrive. Don't waste time waiting for me."

Ricky hung up, turned to Christina, and lamented, "Those assholes won't leave me alone, even on my day off."

He threw the phone down in frustration. Christina didn't know about the desert compound, and Ricky wanted to keep it that way. He told her, "There is an emergency at the Institute hospital. I've got to go help out."

Getting up, he looked longingly down at Christina's naked body then turned and dove into the pool. After one quick lap he climbed out and told her, "I'll be back as soon as I can. It shouldn't take long."

Christina pouted, but knew it was pointless to make a fuss. Instead, she acquiesced and offered, "I'll have lunch ready when you return, but Ricky, please hurry."

He bounded up to the bedroom, took a quick shower, threw on clothes then headed to the garage.

Ricky picked the red Porsche and turned on its ignition. As the clutch engaged, the car lunged forward with only inches separating its roof from the rising garage door. He sped down the driveway and onto the street with wheels screeching. At the first intersection, he turned due west, in the direction of the desert.

3

Ricky Pedraza climbed up the stairs of the white building at the compound. He pressed a code into the keypad. A lock clicked open, and he went inside.

Proceeding down a dimly lit hallway, he came to the only door with light emanating from its window. Ricky pushed the door ajar and stuck his head inside. "Are you ready for me?" he asked.

Don Adams, his surgical technician, looked up from the operative field.

"Give me another minute, and we'll be all set." Adams said with an unmistakable Texas accent.

"What the hell is taking you so long?"

"Come on, Ricky, cut me some slack. This case came out of the clear blue. Look, by the time you change, we'll be good to go."

Ricky brusquely pulled his head out and marched over to the locker room. He took his shirt and slacks off and hung them up with care. Finally, he undid a holster, which held the Beretta strapped above his ankle.

After donning surgical scrubs, he made his way back toward the operating room. At the sink outside, he began the ritual of washing his hands and arms from the elbows down, using a sponge soaked with soapy disinfectant.

With dripping hands held aloft, he pushed the operating room door open with his hip. Inside, the high-pitched whir of a surgical saw drowned out any other sounds. The faint smell of burning flesh hung in the air from use of electric cautery.

"How long has he been on the table?" Ricky asked.

Adams responded, "About twenty-five minutes."

"Who is he?"

"Some guy named Sanchez. Ramon and Hector brought him here this morning." Adams continued, "He must have been in a world of pain before Fernandez put him under."

"What makes you say that?" Pedraza asked from behind his surgical mask.

"Look at his hand."

Ricky saw an arm dangling off the side of the table. The hand had all its fingers cut off above the knuckles. A pool of blood had accumulated on the floor below.

"I suppose they were trying to get a little information before the surgery."

Adams answered, "Probably, but those two assholes used my rib cutters and didn't have the decency to put them in the sterilizer afterward." Ricky had enlisted Adams to come to Mazatlan after working with him at Baylor. As chief surgical technician at Baylor's animal lab, he helped Pedraza hone his skills during training.

Many of the most talented surgeons in the country, who at one time or another were at Baylor, owed a debt of gratitude to Adams for the help he gave them. It was in his lab that young surgeons like Ricky Pedraza had a chance to perfect their technique on animals before working on humans.

Adams had devoted his whole life to the field of surgery, yet he wasn't an MD. Accordingly, he couldn't perform or even assist in the most minor surgical procedures done on patients at Baylor's hospital located directly across the street from his lab.

Although Ricky offered Adams top dollar to work in Mazatlan, it wasn't the money that lured him; it was being able to do what he had always dreamed of—performing surgery on humans.

Ricky trusted Adams both inside and outside the operating room. Adams didn't have any vices that might get him into trouble. Better yet, he never refused anything Ricky asked.

Ricky made a final adjustment to his surgical gown then stepped up to the operating table opposite Adams who already had cut through the patient's sternum and abdominal wall, all the way to the pubic bone. Adams positioned a retractor along the margins of the abdominal incision and cranking its small lever, the arms spread the opening wide. Once there was adequate exposure, Pedraza put one hand deep inside the cavity and felt around to feel size and position of the vital organs. When his exploration was complete Ricky turned to Adams and said, "Okay, *mi amigo* let's get to work."

The two proceeded methodically with their task. Kidneys came out first, then pancreas, and finally the liver. Each organ was carefully placed into its own cooler filled with a special iced preservative solution the color of pink lemonade. During the final stages of the harvest, they left the abdomen, prepared to take heart and lungs from the chest.

Pedraza held a syringe filled with potassium-rich fluid, and injected it into the patient's aorta just above the coronary arteries. Seconds later, the solution flowing into the coronary circulation caused cardiac arrest from ventricular fibrillation. Effective heart contractions ceased and were replaced with small quivering movements incapable of pumping blood. Soon the quivering stopped, and the heart lay perfectly still. Within minutes the heart and lungs were removed and put into their respective containers.

Ricky glanced over the partition at the head of the operating table where the dozing anesthesiologist, Rafael Fernandez, was seated.

"Fernandez!" Ricky called out as the anesthesiologist awoke with a start. "You can turn off the damn ventilator. This operation is over."

What had been a viable human being only hours before was now reduced to the shell of an eviscerated corpse. The entire surgery, from start to finish, was completed in less than two hours.

Ricky turned away from the operating table and began removing his gown. Adams looked toward Dr. Pedraza and said, "I'll take the coolers to the organ bank at the Institute. Ramon and Hector will deal with the body."

Before Dr. Pedraza made his exit, Adams added, "Oh, Ricky, one more thing. I got a call from the island. Gutierrez has some cases and wants us to go there tomorrow."

"Well, fuck him. That money hungry bastard will just have to wait another day. Call the island and tell them to reschedule." There was obvious irritation in Ricky's voice. He went on. "You know, we really could use some more help around here."

Adams listened as Pedraza continued his rant. "For the money we pay, a good surgeon should be easy to find." The surgical technician nodded in agreement.

Ricky went on. "I've got to talk with Jamison. Between the organ harvesting and transplants, there's too much work for the three of us. He'll have to find someone who can do the job and keep his mouth shut at the same time."

Pedraza pushed open the door of the OR, leaving Adams and the corpse emptied of its organs behind. Minutes later, the Porsche was heading back toward the villa and rock music was blasting over the speakers. A smile came to Ricky's face as he drove. He could feel himself getting hard just thinking about Christina's body. He would pick up where he left off when Adams's phone call interrupted him. Lunch could wait.

4

Rob Sanders opened the door to his apartment; it was close to midnight. A note from Sarah lay on the kitchen table.

"I left a plate for you in the refrigerator. Hope you had a good day."

Rob put the paper down, walked over to the fridge and took out his dinner. He was too tired to bother with the microwave. Instead, he picked at the cold food. Most people who start work at six in the morning don't eat dinner at midnight, but for Dr. Rob Sanders it wasn't a rare event.

He scanned the day's mail that lay on the table while he ate. Nothing looked important. After eating, he cautiously tiptoed into his son's bedroom. Standing silently, he looked down at his beautiful sandy haired four-year-old sleeping peacefully. Rob carefully adjusted Josh's blanket. He longed to spend more time with his son. Unfortunately, most days he left for work before Josh was awake and returned home well after his bedtime.

Entering the master bedroom, Rob undressed and stealthily got under the covers so as not to disturb Sarah. He was asleep as soon his head hit the pillow.

At 2 a.m. his pager went off. Rob's arm shot over in the direction of the bleating sound coming from the nightstand. He fumbled with the pager then pressed the button shutting it off. Sarah, asleep at his side, sighed once and turned over, but didn't awaken. Rob squinted to view the pale green numerals on the pager. They belonged to the extension of the surgical intensive care unit at Boston General. He propped himself up on one elbow, reached for the phone, and dialed.

The nurse in the SICU answered his call. "Sorry to wake you, Dr. Sanders," she said, "but can I have an order to give Mrs. Jordan something for her nausea?" Although half-asleep, Rob distinctly recalled logging postoperative orders into the computer including medication for nausea. Rather than chew the nurse out for not checking the orders more carefully, he cleared his throat and said softly, "You can give her eight milligrams of Zofran."

The nurse answered, "Okay, doctor," and the conversation was over.

Rob put down the phone. If he was lucky, he could still get a few hours of uninterrupted sleep before he got up for work.

When Rob had begun Cheryl Jordan's surgery, it had looked like it would be a straightforward kidney transplant. But the routine case turned into a near disaster.

Cheryl Jordan had been on dialysis four years and found the experience intolerable. It required her to drive to a treatment center three times a week and spend six hours connected to a machine in a room with nine other patients each connected to their own unit. Sure, dialysis purified her bloodstream, taking over the function of her failed kidneys, but it took its toll on her, both physically and mentally. She lost weight even though she wasn't heavy to begin with. Usually, when she ran into her friends, they would say, "Cheryl, you look great," but the sallow face she saw when looking in a mirror told her the truth.

Cheryl had a vein graft that lay just beneath the skin of her left forearm. It was into that vein that the nurses inserted the needles that connected her to the dialysis machine. Over time, the vein had enlarged and looked like a pulsating snake. She was disgusted by its appearance.

Cheryl hated dialysis, but needed it to live. Without regular treatments she would go into a coma and die of uremic poisoning. Because of her miserable existence, Cheryl longed for a kidney transplant.

Her prayers were answered the day she got a call from the regional organ transplant center. Her case manager gave her the good news, "Cheryl, we've located a kidney that's an excellent match. Do you think you can make it to Boston General as soon as possible? I expect they'll be able to do your surgery within the next twenty-four hours." For a moment she held the phone speechless, frozen by the news.

"Are you all right?" the case manager asked when there was no response. Finally, she managed to get out, "Yes. Yes, I'm fine. It just took a second for what you said to register." Cheryl's voice was choked by emotion. If the case manager had been nearby, she would have grabbed her and kissed her.

Without delay, she began to organize the few things needed to take with for her hospital stay. She called her husband at his office, telling him to leave work immediately and come pick her up.

Rachel, her teenage daughter, was home from school instant messaging friends on the computer in her bedroom. When Cheryl interrupted her to share the news, Rachel sprang up from her chair and hugged her mother tightly. Within an hour they were heading north on the expressway toward Boston.

The national waiting list for a kidney transplant had over fifty thousand people on it, all desperate to have a new organ, desperate to get off dialysis. Unfortunately, there simply weren't enough organs to go around. The need for donor kidneys far exceeded their availability, and the waiting list was getting longer.

Cheryl's new organ was coming from a man in Rhode Island. He had been declared brain-dead only hours earlier, after two days in a coma. His tissue and blood type were well matched to hers.

The man's compact car was demolished by an SUV that ran a red light. Its driver had stopped to meet some buddies for a few beers on the way home from work. While he escaped with only a bruised knee and some facial abrasions, the occupant of the car didn't fare as well. He suffered severe head trauma and rib fractures. His left lung collapsed from one of the splintered ribs puncturing it. A CT scan showed a skull fracture and areas of intracerebral bleeding. The neurosurgeon who saw him in consultation thought he wouldn't make it through the night.

Once he was pronounced brain dead, consent was obtained from his wife for organ donation. The procurement team was mobilized. They would take as many of his organs as possible. Unfortunately, the trauma had damaged the man's lungs and put excessive strain on his heart so they couldn't be used. The team had to settle for the kidneys, liver, and pancreas.

Cheryl's new organ was flown to Boston by chartered plane then transported by ambulance to the General. The cooler holding the organ looked no different than the kind used for a family picnic. However, containing its lifesaving contents, it was securely belted into the passenger seat.

Cheryl was under anesthesia in the operating room. Marcus Bradford, an African-American general surgical resident rotating on the transplant service, painted her abdominal wall with iodine solution and positioned the sterile drapes that outlined the surgical field. When he wasn't rounding Marcus spent time assisting in the OR.

Dr. Rob Sanders stepped up to the operating table across from Marcus. Rob held out his hand, and a nurse snapped the blunt end of a scalpel onto his palm. His fingers gripped the handle. Rob made an incision about six inches long, through skin then subcutaneous tissue. He proceeded, extending the incision even deeper to the underlying fascia and muscular layer. Finally, using scissors, he gingerly cut the paper-thin layer of peritoneum that allowed entry into the abdominal cavity.

Marcus retracted loops of intestine as Sanders reached down into the pelvis, dissecting a space into which he would eventually position the donated kidney. Suddenly, bright red arterial blood spurted onto Sanders gown and protective glasses.

Rob realized he must have nicked an aberrant arterial branch. He had to find a way to stop the blood gushing from the torn artery.

The surgical nurse reached over and wiped Rob's goggles while Marcus pushed the tip of a suction catheter deep into the bloody surgical field, trying to clear Rob's view.

Mel Howard, the anesthesiologist, started the case in a jovial mood. Moments before, he was humming to the Rolling Stones playing on the operating room's CD player. His demeanor changed when he saw Cheryl's blood pressure plummet. Anticipating the patient would need transfusions, he called for additional units from the blood bank. With a bleeder like this, his patient could go into irreversible shock and die in a matter of minutes. He needed to keep pace with the blood loss. Howard opened up the intravenous lines full blast, administering fluid as quickly as possible.

The staff couldn't see Mel's trembling hands behind the draped barrier at the head of the table. He placed the first unit of blood inside a pressure bag and pumped it in as fast as he could. After the first he put up a second. On the monitor Mel saw Cheryl's blood pressure stop dropping and level off. He felt a little better, but they weren't entirely out of the woods yet. "*Sanders, you've got to get that damned bleeder,*" Mel thought to himself.

Although Marcus tried hard, his suctioning couldn't keep the surgical field clear. Sanders hands were submerged in a pool of red that extended above his wrists.

"Long hemostat," Rob called out. A second later the nurse slapped the instrument handle into Sander's extended palm.

Using his fingertips as eyes, Rob positioned the hemostat tip where he felt the origin of the pulsating bleeder. He took a breath, opened the teeth of his instrument, and clamped onto the tissue. Everyone in the room heard the sound of the hemostat snap shut.

The pulsation at his fingertips stopped. He waited a little longer. Finally, convinced he had clamped the torn arterial branch, Rob announced, "I think we got it."

With the serious complication under control, tension in the room quickly abated. Everyone was smiling beneath their surgical masks, and Mel joyfully exclaimed, "Way to go, Sanders!"

Stability restored, Mel cranked up the volume on the CD player bringing Mick Jagger's Jumpin' Jack Flash back into the operating room.

Dr. William Mayer, a senior transplant surgeon, burst into the operating room. Breathing heavily from his run to the OR, after receiving an emergency page, Mayer asked," Do you need an extra set of hands?"

"Appreciate the offer, Dr Mayer, but we've got things under control."

"Are you sure?"

"I'm sure."

Mayer left the room and Marcus, who had been silent the whole time asked, "I couldn't see a damn thing in there besides blood. How the heck did you get that bleeder?"

As the operation continued, the donor kidney was removed from an Igloo cooler. A nurse placed the pale, ice-cold organ into Marcus's hands. He, in turn, passed it to Rob who positioned it inside Cheryl's pelvic cavity. Rob sutured the donor kidney's artery to the patient's internal iliac artery. Then he allowed Marcus to suture the vein. During the final phase, Rob connected the kidney's ureter to the bladder, so urine had a route to leave the body. When the connections were completed, Rob released the clamp across the artery and allowed bright red, oxygenated blood to flow from the iliac artery into the organ.

He watched as the pale kidney became pink and throbbed with the return of arterial blood. Rob found the sight beautiful to behold. He never tired of seeing life restored to a donor organ.

Finishing in the OR, Rob spoke to Cheryl's family in the waiting area. Then he went into the surgical lounge and sank into the leather sofa positioned directly in front of a big-screen television. The nightly news was on. However, Rob didn't hear a word the broadcaster was saying. Instead, his mind went back to review the surgery just completed. Could he have done anything differently to avoid cutting the aberrant artery? The branch wasn't seen on the preoperative angiogram.

Rob realized how close his patient had come to dying. Sometimes, in a case like this, it was difficult to attribute success to dumb luck or skill. When the teeth of his hemostat clamped onto the arterial bleeder, which factor was responsible? It was impossible for him to answer for certain, but the only thing that mattered now was that his patient and her new kidney were doing fine.

5

Salvador Gutierrez was standing at the dock alongside his SUV when Ricky and Adams arrived. In two hours, *El Scalpel* had brought them to Maria Madre, an island roughly 110 miles southwest off the coast form Mazatlan.

Maria Madre served as a penal colony since 1905. It was once known as the Mexican Alcatraz, but in recent times its prisoners were treated more humanely. No longer did they expect to die there and rot in the sun.

The weather that morning was perfect for the trip, but Ricky knew the forecast and noted storm clouds on the horizon. They would have to work fast and try to get out before the weather turned. The last thing he wanted was to be stuck on the island with Gutierrez and his gang of juiced-up prison guards.

Adams started unloading Igloo containers from the hold while Ricky took his briefcase, disembarked, and walked forward to meet his smiling host. Gutierrez held out his hand. The warden typically didn't bother picking them up, sending one of his lackeys instead.

"Dr. Ricky, I'm so glad you came. I was afraid the forecast might scare you away."

"Sal, thanks for your concern, but I plan to be long gone when the weather hits."

Inside the SUV Gutierrez spoke first, "I trust your father is in good health?"

"Luis is fine and sends his best."

"Wonderful. Here, I have a little gift for him." The warden handed Ricky a box of fine Cuban cigars. "These are his favorites," he said then added, "Did you happen to bring an envelope for me?" he asked.

"Yes, of course."

Ricky opened his briefcase, took out the large manila envelope stuffed with hundred-dollar bills and handed it to him.

"Ah. Very nice," the warden said, his eyes widening as he viewed the payment. Gutierrez turned to Ricky then asked, "And the rest?"

Ricky reached back into the briefcase and pulled out a package of cocaine telling Gutierrez, "There's more than enough here to keep your guards happy for the next few weeks."

The warden's smile broadened, as he clutched the bag of white powder.

"I thank you and your father. Unfortunately, I must be frank. Our expenses have increased considerably over the last few months. In order for me to keep my staff happy and assure you a steady supply of organs, we will need 10 percent more on the next visit."

Not willing to make a commitment before conferring with his father, Ricky answered, "I'll pass along your request. I'm sure an arrangement can be worked out." Then he changed the subject. "I heard you had a problem with one of the donors after he was released."

"Yes, the idiot got drunk and talked too much. Of course, we found him and brought him right back. To set an example I took him deep sea fishing."

"You took him fishing? Are you crazy?"

Gutierrez started laughing. "*Compadre*, relax. I didn't give him a fishing pole and a beer. We tied some heavy line around his waist, cut him up a little so he bled, and then threw him overboard. The sharks came in a matter of minutes and started nibbling. We hauled what was left back and laid it out in the yard for the other prisoners to view. I guarantee you that none of them will ever speak about what happens on this island."

Adams finished loading the last of the coolers into the SUV's rear and shut the hatch. He got into the back seat and Gutierrez drove them off. They drove to the island infirmary. The patients were already under anesthesia awaiting surgery.

6

The alarm went off at 5:30 a.m. Rob got up and readied for the day ahead. He threw his lab coat on and grabbed a banana heading out the door for the hospital. His first case was scheduled at 7 a.m., which didn't leave much time to round with his team of medical students and residents. He would try to see the sickest patients first, before being called away to the operating room.

Rob got a coffee in the hospital lobby. He took an elevator and exited on the fourth floor. He walked a short distance down the corridor and swiped his ID card across a sensor on the wall. The doors to Boston General's Surgical Intensive Care Unit opened.

The SICU was an alien world. It lacked exterior windows and was illuminated by fluorescent lights. The sounds of beeping monitors and whooshing respirators were everywhere. As the work day began, human voices added to the mechanical din. It was hardly a restful environment, but most of the patients were in a peacefully comatose state induced by intravenous sedation. Every once in a while, a patient would lighten up and begin to stir. An increase in the infusion rate of propofol settled the patient back into sound artificial slumber.

Like a Las Vegas casino, you couldn't easily discern the time. The most accurate way to tell day from night was by the nursing staff. They worked in shifts so that the faces of the nurses present gave some indication whether it was morning, afternoon, or evening.

Rob walked to the far end of the unit and pushed open a door marked "Conference Room." The three medical students and two residents seated around a table in the center looked up at him. Each held a wad of papers containing the results of lab tests, body scans, and X-rays on their assigned patients.

Rob set his cup of coffee down on the table and said with a smile, "Morning, everyone."

While the team members hurriedly finished organizing their information Rob asked, "So, how'd we do last night?"

Jason Liu, the resident who had been on call, answered. He had already polished off his second cup of coffee, the Styrofoam containers sitting empty in front of him. Jason showed the signs of a night on call. His scrubs were badly wrinkled, hair disheveled, and he had a burgeoning growth of facial stubble. In spite of his appearance, the clarity of his voice and manner showed he was in full control of his faculties.

"It wasn't too bad," Jason answered. "Everybody on our list yesterday is still here today. We did have a little trouble from Mr. Watkins in bed six. Around 3 a.m. he became combative and pulled out his endotracheal tube. Luckily, I got one back down and reconnected him to the ventilator before he went flatline."

Jason went down the list of transplant patients and, together with the medical student responsible for knowing the details of the most current lab results, gave a status report on each one.

After the team finished report, they left the conference room and began making rounds, visiting patients at their bedside. As the group walked through the SICU, Rob stopped outside Cheryl Jordan's room. "What's with Mrs. Jordan?" Rob inquired.

Jason responded, "Her hemoglobin remained stable during the night. She's making plenty of urine, and the BUN is steadily improving. All in all, I'd say the patient and her new kidney are doing very well."

The postoperative transplant cases routinely stayed in the SICU for the first forty-eight hours for close monitoring. Once stability was assured, they were transferred out to regular floor wards for further recuperation. As the morning progressed, some in the group would split off to help in the operating room. For the medical students, that usually meant holding retractors. The surgical residents, Jason and especially Marcus, were allowed to do some of the cutting and suturing. As a senior transplant fellow, Rob was the primary operator and did the surgeries from start to finish with a senior attending as backup if he needed it.

When they were at a bedside, team members examined the patient. They changed dressings, pulled out drains and put in central venous lines. They looked over diagnostic studies like CT scans or chest X-rays, checked vital signs, urine flow, and blood work. Finally, they made decisions about which medications should be given or tests performed and wrote orders in the patient's chart.

People came to Boston General because it had the reputation as the best that modern medicine had to offer. Most of the patients were of modest means and like Cheryl Jordan came from the surrounding region. However, some were very wealthy and traveled from other states or foreign countries. During the course of his fellowship, Rob had cared for a number of rich VIPs. It was not unusual that, in an expression of gratitude, some had made the donation of a considerable amount of money to the institution. Nearly everywhere you looked along the walls of the hospital's corridors there were plaques acknowledging the names of benefactors.

Rob remembered the case of Abdul Mahafsah. The Sheikh needed a transplant for chronic hepatitis that slowly ate away at his liver. He could have gone anywhere in the world to get a new organ, but decided the General was where he wanted the surgery and that the department head, Tom Ryan, should be the one to do it.

The size of the entourage that accompanied the Sheikh from Dubai astounded Rob. A group of forty, including four veiled wives and fourteen children, came along. They landed at Logan in their private 747. A caravan of stretch limos transported the group to accommodations at the Four Seasons, where the top two floors were reserved in advance as residence.

Sheik Mahafsah had his transplant two days later and had an uneventful recovery. The day he was preparing to leave hospital, Rob stopped by his room to make sure discharge plans were in order, but Dr. Ryan was already there. Rob stood by and watched the interaction that took place. The sheikh spoke in Arabic, and his aide acted as interpreter.

"Dr. Ryan, you have given me my life back, and for this I am eternally grateful. May it be Allah's will that you visit me in Dubai and enjoy my hospitality."

Ryan answered, "Thank you for your kind offer, but my patients and busy schedule leave me with little time for travel."

The Sheikh whispered to his aide who then took a briefcase lying on the nearby chair and brought it over.

The aide spoke, "Sheik Mahafsah wishes to present you with a token gift in thanks for all your efforts." He slowly opened the briefcase, revealing stacks of hundred-dollar bills completely filling the inside.

Rob estimated that there was at least several hundred thousand dollars in front of him, enough to pay off the massive debt he still had from his educational loans and then some.

Dr. Ryan looked at the money and said to the aide, "Please inform the Sheikh that I cannot personally accept his generous gift. However, if he so desires, I could arrange that his gift be applied toward our departmental research fund. In that way he can ensure that progress in transplantation science will continue well into the future."

The assistant translated Ryan's words and the Sheikh nodded in understanding. Then he said something more to his aide, who in turn addressed Ryan.

"The Sheikh will do as you wish."

Sheikh Mahafsah stood up, placed his right hand over his heart, and then bowed graciously to Dr. Ryan, who in kind bowed back. The scene was one Rob would never forget.

7

Rob Sanders's origins were in the Midwest. He went to college at the University of Illinois then medical school and surgical residency at Northwestern. His chief of surgery, Chip Foster, recognized Rob's talent and took a special interest in him. Foster was an alumnus of Boston General, where he built the national reputation that ultimately garnered his position as department head in Chicago.

The transplant fellowship at the General was regarded as one of the best in the world. While Rob had excellent credentials, so did the scores of other applicants. In the end it was Foster's sterling letter of recommendation that got Rob his spot in the program. Nothing helped more to nail down a position at an elite training program than personal advocacy from a notable alumnus.

Rob's father never received a high school diploma. He left school to take a job with the railroad and worked there his entire adult life. Rob was the only one in the family who went to college. While there, he became interested in science, especially biochemistry and immunology. Rob took a chance and applied to medical school not really thinking he would be accepted. However, with his outstanding grades and a top score on the medical school entrance exam he got in.

Rob met Sarah as a second-year resident, and she was working the night shift on one of the surgical wards. One of her patients had soaked through his surgical dressing with blood. She paged the resident on call, Rob Sanders.

When Rob came to check on the situation, he was impressed by Sarah's pleasant smile, chestnut-brown hair, and her shapely figure that wasn't totally hidden by the tawdry nursing uniform. She took note of him as well. Rob stood five-foot-eleven, had blue eyes and broad shoulders. Their hands touched as he helped her replace the dressing, causing Sarah to blush. Afterward, Rob lingered on the ward with the excuse he wanted to keep a close eye on the patient, but the only thing he kept his eye on was Sarah. He talked with her at the nursing station for the better part of that night.

Less than a year later, they were married. The wedding took place in her hometown of Dayton, Ohio. At the time Rob was twenty-seven, and the only material things he had to his name were a few stacks of medical books and some secondhand furniture.

Neither could rely on any financial support from their families, plus Rob was in debt from educational loans. They talked about starting a family, but wondered how they would make ends meet. Rob needed to do something to generate additional income. He began working at emergency rooms on the nights he wasn't on call at his hospital. Being up most of the night several times a week left Rob so fatigued that, at times, he was barely able to drag himself from bed. However, it was this moonlighting income that kept them from sinking any deeper into debt than they already were.

When Rob was accepted for the transplant fellowship in Boston, there was a minor hitch—the job there meant a cut in his salary. It seemed that the privilege of training at one of the most venerable medical institutions in the world demanded a financial sacrifice. In spite of the unfavorable economics, they decided he should take the position.

Rob and Sarah were invited to visit Boston at the department's invitation. Sarah's father, Randy Martin, a retired Air Force colonel and her mother flew in from Dayton so they could babysit for Josh.

On their first morning in Boston, Sarah and Rob took a walking tour of the city that began at Boston Common. They had an early lunch at the oldest restaurant in the city, the Union Oyster House. Afterward they took in the sights around Quincy Market and Faneuil Hall.

That night, alone in their hotel room at the Parker House, they had a perfect opportunity for some overdue intimacy. In the seasoned old hotel marked by stately Yankee tradition, Sarah and Rob made love with a feverish intensity that surprised them both. Afterward, lying in the darkness, their heavy breathing was the only audible sound.

"Not bad for an old married couple," she whispered in his ear.

"You were absolutely amazing," Rob told her. Within minutes, both fell into a contented sleep.

On the second day of their visit, they looked into living arrangements. Visiting different neighborhoods they discovered the cost of renting an apartment in Boston was even higher than in Chicago. Fortunately, the hospital offered subsidized housing for its medical staff on campus. The decision made, Rob signed a lease for an apartment that provided a not so scenic view of the General's gray limestone exterior less than one hundred yards away.

8

As Rob and his transplant team were rounding in the ICU, they crossed paths with the trauma service. Scott Harper, a senior trauma fellow, who had his own group of residents and medical students in tow, emerged from room eight. The team members had no smiles and filed quietly from the room, each one wearing a look of disappointment on their face.

One of Rob's residents, Jason Liu, couldn't pass by the door without looking in. Jason wasn't nosey, just insatiably curious from the medical point of view to find out what was going on. He slowed his step then broke away from his transplant team and peaked into room eight. Jason saw the patient on a ventilator with his eyes taped shut. The only part of him moving was his chest, which went up and down to the cadence of the ventilator, intermittently inflating his lungs. Jason approached a friend of his, Arnie Jaffe, a resident rotating on trauma.

"Say, Arnie, what's with the patient you got in there?"

"Talk about bad luck. The poor guy was minding his own business, working at a construction site. A nail gun jammed, and he tried to get it working. Somehow it went off and he got hit in the head."

"Tough break," Jason observed.

"Yeah, chalk it up to fucking bad karma. He was probably brain dead when he hit the ER yesterday, no reflexes, and both pupils were fixed and dilated. CT of his head showed the nail lodged deep inside white matter, turning most of his brain tissue into mush."

Arnie pointed to the tubing emerging from the top of the patient's skull, which was hooked to a pressure monitor. "The numbers for his intracranial pressure are off the charts. Nobody around here has ever seen an ICP that high. Harper just declared him officially brain dead. Now I've got to go tell family the bad news and ask them about organ donation." Arnie continued, "For the time being, we're giving him lots of intravenous fluids, and a levophed drip to help keep his blood pressure up. If family says no, we stop the drips, disconnect the vent and cart his body off to the morgue. If they say yes, you'll get a call to take his heart, lungs, kidneys, pancreas, and liver."

While Jason was speaking with Arnie, the rest of the transplant team had progressed down the corridor. The group was starting to discuss Daryl Freeman, in room twelve, when Rob noticed Jason halfway down the hall. He motioned for him to hurry up and rejoin the group. Jason hustled back to his team. The stethoscope and reflex hammer stuffed into the pocket of his lab coat almost fell out as he ran.

Mr. Freeman was a thirty-eight-year-old kidney transplant patient who was receiving high doses of immune system suppressants because of an early rejection reaction. Unfortunately, he had developed a fever of 104 and was desperately ill. The infectious disease specialists were brought in to consult and suspected that a fungus, *Candida albicans,* was responsible. They ordered the antifungal medication that was dripping into his intravenous line.

Freeman brought back to Rob's mind the case of one another transplant patient who succumbed to infection. At autopsy, he saw that all major organs were loaded with multiple craters filled with chocolate syrup–looking liquid. The *Aspergilla* fungus had literally eaten his patient to death!

After that, any time Rob heard that one of his patients developed a high fever he became concerned. It was one of the most frustrating aspects of his job, putting in all that effort to get sick patients through transplant surgery only to lose them later on to infection.

After leaving Freeman's bedside, the team headed out of the SICU and over to the surgical wards. They visited Gerald Fitch Sr. and his son. The father had chronic hepatitis, which turned him a sickly yellowish-brown color from the bile build up in his body.

As his liver problems progressed, the need for a transplant became more urgent, yet he was nowhere near the top of the registry list. Fitch's son decided he had to help his father, so Gerald Jr. offered himself set up as a living donor. The father and son were both undergoing final preparation for their simultaneous surgery.

The procedure involved removing a small portion of the left lobe of Gerald Jr.'s liver not much bigger than a fist. The segment of liver would be placed in a stainless steel bowl of preservative solution and carried from his operating room over to his father's next door. The senior Fitch's abdomen would already be been open, prepared to receive the transplant. After a few hours, the dual surgeries would be complete.

Gerald Jr. had agreed to be a donor even though he was told there were risks. Rob wanted to go over things one final time before the operation.

"I want to be sure you understand there are some serious complications that could arise from your operation," Rob told the son.

"Well, Doc, you can tell me again if you want to, but we went over all that stuff before in the clinic."

"You're right, but that was a couple of weeks ago. Just bear with me for a minute, and let's go through it again."

"Whatever."

"First, there could be bleeding in your abdomen postoperatively, and we might have to take you back to the operating room or give you a transfusion. Then you could get a wound infection or develop pneumonia during recovery. Occasionally, a blood clot will form in the leg veins and travel up into the lungs, causing a pulmonary embolism. Any or all those things could happen, and even though it would be unlikely, you could die as a result."

"No big deal so far, doc. I trust you."

"It's not just about trust. It's about complications that can happen even in the best of hands. Your surgery is entirely elective and has nothing to do with any illness or problem you have. You're a perfectly healthy guy."

In spite of the risks, Gerald Jr. took the consent forms and signed them.

"Doc, let me tell you something about my dad. We did everything together when I was a kid. He didn't make much money, but he found a way for us to see the Red Sox play whenever we got a chance. There's nothing better than being at Fenway. We still try to go every once in a while, although now with his being sick and all it isn't easy. I'm not ready to let all that become a memory and watch him continue decaying in front of my eyes. If he needs a piece of my liver to help him out, it's his."

"I know what you mean," Rob said. As the words came from his lips, he thought about his own father.

The image in his mind was of a half-smoked cigarette hanging from his dad's lips. Although a doctor, Rob was powerless in the face of his father's addiction to nicotine. He kept right on smoking even after the diagnosis of lung cancer. Rob would have gladly donated a kidney or piece of liver if that would have solved his father's problem. In the end, only death separated him from his cigarettes.

Rob's pager went off. They were nearly ready to begin the Fitch cases. Rob and Marcus set off for the OR, while the rest of the team continued rounding with Jason.

A living donor-liver transplant relied on the unique capacity of hepatic cells to regenerate. Only a relatively small portion of healthy liver was needed for the transplant since the implanted segment would grow in size to take over for the failing organ. The donor's remaining liver would also grow over time to replace its missing portion.

Adjoining operating suites were set up. Rob, with Marcus assisting, worked on the son while Dr. Mayer operated on the senior Fitch in the room next door. The father's cirrhotic organ was a shriveled mass of dysfunctional scarred tissue. Mayer removed most of the diseased left lobe. The segment of his son's healthy liver would be sutured into that location.

Once Rob removed a portion of the son's liver he delicately placed it in a bowl of preservative solution. A nurse walked it over to the OR next door.

Rob let Marcus finish up with the case. He took off his gown and gloves then rescrubbed to assist Mayer with the father's surgery. When the operation was over, Rob paged Jason to get an update on how rounds were going, then he briefly called Sarah to say hi.

Tomorrow was Rob's research day. Each week, he spent one full day working at the research building adjacent to the hospital. His research day was a time of welcome relief from dealing with the life and death issues on clinical service. It was the one day he could expect to make it home for dinner even if he had to go back afterward and finish up.

Rob was completing a project he had been working on for months. His research involved an antibody that blocked a receptor on rabbit white cells. He would inject the antibody just prior to giving the rabbit a transplanted kidney. In the control animals, the new kidney was destroyed in a matter of days. But so far, administering the blocking antibody seemed to prevent the rejection reaction from occurring.

Rob's goal was to be able to induce a state of tolerance in his experimental rabbits. If his antibody worked well in rabbits, it might work in humans and that could mean a breakthrough in the way transplant patients were treated.

Rob looked forward to a day when he wouldn't have to worry about infections in his patients because of the immune suppressant drugs they were required to receive. He was convinced there was a better way to deal with the recipient's immune system than poisoning it with drugs like prednisone, cyclosporine, azathioprine, or mycophenolic acid.

His motivation wasn't winning a Nobel Prize or making a fortune by selling the rights to a successful discovery. He just never again wanted to stand by watching a pathologist perform an autopsy on one of his patients who had been ravaged by an overwhelming infection.

9

That evening, when Rob entered his apartment, he found Sarah asleep on the sofa with a book she was reading at her side. Sarah told Rob that while Josh was young, she wanted to be the best possible mother. However, one day, she wanted to go back to school and get a degree in public health.

On weekday mornings Sarah got up early, dressed and fed Josh, and then dropped him off at preschool. From there, she would drive to work at Dr. Jensen's office where she set up his patients until late in the afternoon. After that she would pick Josh up and run whatever errands needed to be done before returning home to make dinner.

When Rob got up the next day, Sarah and Josh were already gone. It was his research day so he got up later than usual. Rob made some breakfast and had coffee before walking over to the research building. As Rob got off the elevator and headed down the hall leading toward his office, he could hear the sounds of barking dogs and screeching monkeys coming from the other labs.

Rob spent the morning processing slides of his research rabbits' kidney tissue and analyzing them during the afternoon. So far his results were looking positive for the effect of the experimental antibody.

At five-thirty his cell phone rang. It was Sarah, and Rob heard her sobbing. "What's wrong?" He asked.

"There's been an accident," Sarah told him.

"Are you and Josh all right?"

"We were shaken up a bit, but thankfully not hurt. I was pulling out of the supermarket when a car broadsided the van. It was damaged pretty badly and had to be towed."

"I'll come get you," Rob offered.

"I've already called a cab, and it should be here anytime. I'll meet you back at the apartment."

Rob headed back home and anxiously awaited their arrival. Sarah came through the door with Josh sleeping on her shoulder.

Her first words were, "How are we going to afford this?" Unable to keep her emotions in check, tears streamed down her face.

Rob tried to put things in perspective. "Thank God, you and Josh are okay. That's the important thing. Our insurance will cover the cost of the repairs."

Sarah was not reassured. "The van will probably take weeks to fix. We'll have to rent a car in the meantime so I can go to work and take Josh to school. Our deductible is a thousand dollars. Between the repairs and the rental, it'll wipe out everything we've got in savings."

Rob hadn't given recent thought to the state of their finances, but Sarah was right. The accident was going to drain their bank account. Of his friends who went into business, most already had their own house. Some were even putting away money for their children's college education. For all his degrees and acknowledgments, he had next to nothing of material value to show for it.

With the end of his training in sight, Rob had lined up several job opportunities. Three well regarded, university transplant programs offered him a position as junior attending and he had to make a choice among them. The salary he would get as an academic surgeon would never approach what he could make in private practice. Removing gallbladders, repairing hernias, and doing breast biopsies all day long could be a lot more lucrative than doing transplantation. Rob knew there would be no fancy car or vacation home in his immediate future, but he would make a decent living and eventually be able to pay down the debt that hung over his head.

The perks to an academic practice were nonmonetary. He would be able to continue doing research, writing papers, and attending meetings of the professional societies he belonged to. It was at those gatherings that the results of the latest research were presented. In fact, a few months back, Rob had spent several days in Florence at the International College of Transplantation meeting. It was his first time out of the country, and Boston General covered the cost of the trip.

Rob had to wonder whether the four years of college, four years of medical school, five years residency, and three years of fellowship were worth it.

Sarah stopped her sobbing as Rob contemplated the painful reality of their finances. Rob thought, *Only a few more months to go. Things have got to be better with the salary of a junior attending.* The rest of the evening passed in silence, until they finally went to bed.

The next day while making rounds, he received a page from Sarah. Although it wasn't like him to be pessimistic, he had the feeling it was going to be more bad news.

"Rob, were you expecting a FedEx letter?"

"No. Who sent it?"

"The label says it's from the Jamison Institute."

"The Jamison Institute," Rob repeated. "I've never heard of the place. I'll check it out later when I get home." He asked what was weighing on his mind, "Did you find anything new out about the van?"

"Yes, and it's not good. The estimate for repairs is $3,800." She answered with sadness in her voice.

That evening Rob sat dejected by the kitchen table. He picked up the FedEx envelope in front of him and opened it. What he found inside caused more than a little surprise. The letter was written by Pat Hurley, administrator of the Jamison Institute in Mazatlan, Mexico. Rob was invited to visit the facility and bring his family along, all expenses paid. As he read through the body of the letter, he thought he must have made a mistake and reread it. But, there was no mistake. Hurley offered him a staff position doing transplant surgery at the Institute with a starting salary of $350 thousand plus benefits!

The last vacation they had taken as a family was when they spent Josh's first Christmas in Ohio at Sarah's parents'. The thought of going to Mexico for free seemed too good to be true.

Imagine a salary like that. I could pay off my loans in no time and still have enough left over to make a down payment on a house. Sarah wouldn't have to work unless she wanted to, and—Rob stopped his daydreaming. He didn't know a thing about the Institute. He had to find out more about it. Maybe his chief, Tom Ryan, knew of the place and could advise him. Rob was determined to make an appointment with him first thing in the morning.

10

Rob entered Dr. Ryan's office. The department chairman took off his reading glasses and stood up to greet his senior transplant fellow. "Come on in Rob and have a seat." Extending his arm across the massive desk cluttered with journals, he shook Rob's hand firmly.

Tom Ryan was one of the top transplant surgeons in the world. Mounted on the wall behind him was a picture of a much younger Ryan standing with the South African surgeon, Christian Barnard who, in 1967, performed the first successful heart transplant. Another photo had Ryan alongside the president of the United States. Dr. Ryan was a member of the select group of distinguished physicians summoned to meet with the President and discuss issues related to stem cell research, organ transplantation, and cloning. He was also the current editor-in-chief of the field's main journal, *Transplantation Science* as well as President of the American Association of Transplant Surgeons.

These days Ryan did less surgery and spent more of his time traveling around the world, lecturing, and managing the hospital's Department of Surgery Research Foundation. Rob wasn't privy to the details, but he knew that the DSRF had an enormous annual budget. Rob's lab was but a miniscule part of the General's high-powered research machine. The Foundation had relationships with government and industry plus endowments from wealthy benefactors.

Among the important research projects was an attempt to clone organs from a patient's own stem cells. That was a sure way to avoid the possibility of rejection and the need for dangerous immune-suppressive treatment. While there were great hopes for using stem cells in this manner, the investigation was still in its early stage. It would take millions of dollars and more years of hard work to harness the potential of stem cells for the purpose of organ cloning.

In spite of his lofty credentials, Rob had always found Dr. Ryan approachable. He wasn't full of himself the way a renowned chairman at the General might be expected to behave. Ryan was a man Rob felt he could trust and whose counsel was valued. In spite of his many responsibilities, Ryan met regularly with Rob, his senior fellow, to discuss the clinical service as well as his research.

Ryan began the conversation. "How's your project with the antibody coming along?"

"It's going well," Rob answered. "I should have this phase of the project wrapped up soon. I'm analyzing specimens of the transplanted rabbit kidneys, and so far it's looking like the antibody is helping blunt the rejection reaction."

"What about the cytokine measurements?"

"Blood levels of cytokines remained quite low in the treated animals, supporting the antirejection activity of the white cell receptor blockade."

"That's good news," Ryan responded. "I'm delighted to hear it. I certainly hope you'll be able to pull together enough data so it can be presented at the next meeting of the American Society of Transplant Surgery."

"I'm hoping to," Rob answered.

Ryan was aware that his senior fellow was amid the decision of where he should go once his training ended. Updated frequently by his secretary, Virginia, Ryan knew about the offers from Northwestern and the Cleveland Clinic.

The chief cleared his throat and asked, "Have you given more thought about whether you might accept the position as attending in our department?"

"Well, Dr. Ryan, that's the reason I'm here today. I was honored by the offer to join on staff. However, Sarah's family is from Dayton, and it would be nice for her to have them closer by. If I took an offer anywhere else, it would probably be in Cleveland for that reason, but I still haven't made a final decision."

"I fully understand you've got to do what makes most sense for you and your family. The toughest decisions are usually the ones between good options. I will say that you'll be sorely missed if you leave us. Our loss would be Cleveland or Chicago's gain."

"Thanks, Dr. Ryan, it's so kind of you to say that. But there's an opportunity, which came up recently I'd like to run by you.

"Of course, Rob, it's my pleasure."

"Well Dr. Ryan, I received a letter from a place called the Jamison Institute. They've invited me to visit for an interview regarding a position as transplant surgeon. I'd never heard of the place so I thought I might ask you."

Ryan's countenance changed. He looked dismayed. "Well I've never been there myself, so I can't give you any first-hand opinion, however, I've heard they do a fair number of organ transplants and cater to an exclusive clientele." Ryan paused for a moment before continuing, "The Institute was founded by Dr. Hal Jamison who once worked here at Boston General. Hal was a talented surgeon and also a brilliant researcher. We used to be friends. He did pioneering work in the area of long-term organ preservation, which opened the possibility that some day hearts and livers could be stored for weeks in an organ bank, the way we do with blood transfusions.

Then, about five years ago, Hal disappeared without a trace. At the time he was involved in a bitter malpractice suit. The case was settled out of court, but Hal took it hard, and I imagine that had a lot to do with why he left." Ryan's brow furled. "Rob, with all the excellent opportunities in front of you, I hope you're not seriously considering Mexico."

Rob didn't want to tell Ryan about the amazing salary offer or discuss his dire financial straits. Instead he responded, "No sir, but taking my family with me on a trip there while I interview is tempting. We haven't had a decent vacation since Josh was born."

"Well, Rob, I suppose there's no harm in that. If you decide to go, give Jamison my best."

Getting up to take Ryan's hand, Rob thanked him for his time and walked out.

Early in the morning, ten days after his conversation with Ryan, the Sanders family was picked up by limo, transported to Logan Airport, and dropped off at the corporate terminal. Their jet had a logo of the Jamison Institute on its fuselage.

Welcomed on board by the crew, they were the flight's only passengers. Soon after getting buckled in, the jet taxied down the runway and took off.

Josh quickly fell asleep. Rob and Sarah never felt so important. The dwindling bank account and recent accident weren't on Rob's mind. Instead he was thinking about enjoying a well-deserved vacation with his family as guests of the Jamison Institute and not having to pay anything for the experience.

11

As the jet approached for landing, Rob and Sarah were treated to a breathtaking view of the region surrounding Mazatlan. The plane swung out over the Pacific before turning inland then flew over a strip of beach lined by palms.

Sarah gripped Rob's hand with excitement as the door to the jet opened. When they exited the plane, a car was waiting for them. The driver was Mexican but spoke excellent English.

"Welcome," he said with a smile. "My name is Jorge, and I will be taking you to your villa." As they were entering the car, Rob noticed one other plane, a smaller propeller craft, parked at the airfield.

"Say, Jorge, why are things so quiet here? I expected Mazatlan to have a busy airport, with all the tourist traffic you must get."

Jorge answered, "But, Dr. Sanders, this is not the city's airport. This airfield belongs to the Jamison Institute." Both Sarah and Rob exchanged looks of bewilderment. They wondered what kind of hospital owned its own jet and airfield.

In the car Rob and Sarah reviewed the itinerary sent by the Institute. They were to spend a few hours getting settled at the villa. At 7 p.m., they would be picked up to meet Pat Hurley and Dr. Jamison for dinner.

Jorge's car slowed as he approached a gated residential area off the main road. A guard at the entrance permitted his car to pass. Jorge explained to Sarah and Rob that most everyone who worked at the Institute lived inside the community they just entered.

On the way to their villa, they drove down a tree-shaded avenue. The landscaping was immaculate. The community was located on a tract of land along the coast just north of the city. As the car drove deeper into the complex, Rob caught glimpses of the ocean. Finally, Jorge pulled up the driveway leading to the villa where they would be spending the week.

Exiting the car, Gloria Ortega, their housekeeper, met them and introduced herself. Before leaving, Jorge gave Rob his cell-phone number.

"Dr. Sanders, call me if you need anything. Ah, one more thing. There's a Land Rover parked in your garage. The keys are inside." He went on. "If you want to explore Mazatlan on your own, feel free to use it. Otherwise, phone me, and I'll drive you anywhere you want."

Rob felt like he was living an episode of *Fantasy Island,* the television series he had watched as a kid. Episodes began with a group of guests arriving at an enchanted island. They were promised that, while visiting, their fondest dream would come true. What Rob was experiencing now seemed just like that only it wasn't make-believe; it was real.

When the luggage was put away, Gloria walked them through the villa. There was a spectacular view of the ocean from the master suite balcony on the second floor. Outside, the back yard had a swimming pool filled with crystal-blue water. They took a path at the far end of the yard, which penetrated a line of palms leading onto a pristine beach. Gentle ocean waves were rolling in only yards from where they stood.

Heading back to the villa, Gloria began going over the kitchen in detail. Rob made a quick exit. He bounded up the stairs to the bedroom, took off his clothes, and got into a swim-suit. He couldn't remember the last time he'd put it on. Just as quickly, he was back downstairs diving into the pool. Entering the water, Rob felt a million miles from Boston. No thought of antibody receptors, sick patients or bills; he was simply relaxing and enjoying himself.

Rob swam laps and, when he was done, took a long hot shower. Meanwhile, Sarah freshened up and started getting ready for the dinner party that evening.

At precisely 7 p.m. Jorge returned and drove them to Jamison's estate. Jorge punched a code into a keypad at the entrance, signaling the wrought iron gate to open, and the car proceeded up the long driveway lined by elegant royal palms.

As Rob and Sarah exited the car, a servant waited at the entryway. "Dr. Jamison welcomes you to his home. Please follow me if you would."

Beyond the entry they were led through an enormous outdoor alcove that extended well in front of the house.

Proceeding down the serpentine path, they saw a peacock strutting regally off to one side. Other species of exotic birds flew overhead.

A man and woman were walking toward them. As they met on the path, the woman was first to speak.

"Welcome to Mazatlan," she said. "We're so glad you were able to come. I'm Patricia Hurley, but please call me Pat, and this is Dr. Hal Jamison."

Perhaps it was a reflection of chauvinism, but Rob had assumed the administrator, Pat Hurley, was a man. The realization that the Institute's administrator was a Patricia and not a Patrick caught him off guard. Rob guessed her age to be late thirties, and she was stunning. Hurley had blond hair cut short, an athletic build, and wore an elegant evening dress.

Hal Jamison was an imposing man, taller than Rob, who looked remarkably fit for someone who was Ryan's contemporary. Rob noticed some gray invading at his temples.

"Welcome to our home," Jamison said as he shook Rob's hand. "I hope you will find your stay here pleasant as well as informative."

"Dr. Jamison, thank you for inviting us." Rob said, glancing toward Sarah. He went on. "Both of us are very much looking forward to this."

Inside, Rob and Sarah were presented with glasses of champagne. After the first round, Jamison told them, "Please, this evening is meant for you to relax and feel at home. Jorge is driving, so have another if you like." They each took another glass from the silver platter held out by a servant. Jamison led Rob onto the veranda where they continued their conversation while Pat and Sarah stayed inside.

"Let me answer any questions you might have," Pat offered.

"Well, what's the school system like?" Josh's education was the single most relevant issue for her.

Pat explained, "The Institute has developed its own unique educational program. There are over one hundred children enrolled here, the sons and daughters of Institute employees. English is the primary language, but at least one foreign language is required. The plan for each student is individually designed to meet their academic needs."

"That sounds very impressive," Sarah said.

"Well, one of the reasons our facility has attracted such an excellent group of employees," Pat told Sarah, "is that we made quality education of the staffs' children a top priority."

"How old are your children?" Sarah asked.

"We don't have any children," Pat answered. "Hal and I aren't married."

"Sorry, but I thought—"

"No, that's okay. Hal and I go back a long way together, and we have a special affection for each other, but our busy professional lives wouldn't do justice to raising a family. Although we have no children, I can assure you the parents who do are uniformly happy with our program. No expense has been spared pulling together all the elements that provide the children here an exceptional education. Those who have graduated are now attending some of the best universities around the globe."

"Well, Josh is a long way from attending university, but I can't tell you how happy I am to hear what you said." Sarah smiled contentedly.

As Rob and his host made small talk outdoors, Jamison asked, "Why don't you tell me a little about the research you're doing using that antibody of yours?"

Rob was floored. How did Jamison know about the work going on in his lab, three thousand miles away?

Jamison saw the quizzical look on Rob's face. "Don't be surprised," Hal said with a smile. "While the Institute is located far from the hubs of academic medicine like Boston, we make it our business to stay on top of all the current research. When you presented your data in Florence, my colleague, George Fleming, who you'll meet later on during your visit, was in the audience. He listened closely to what you had to say, and I might add, spoke highly of the potential contribution your work represents."

"Thank you, Dr. Jamison," Rob said.

"Knowing your dedication to research, I'm sure you'll appreciate it when I tell you that scientific investigation at the Institute is a top priority." Jamison added with pride, "Our Institute, like Boston General, has important relationships with pharmaceutical companies as well as a number of 'benefactors' who support our facility and its research efforts."

Hal continued as he took a sip from his glass of champagne. "Rob, you shouldn't have the least concern about continuing your current research or even exploring an entirely new avenue of work should you join our staff. At the Institute, we don't have the hassle of applying for NIH grants then praying to be the one that gets funded. Just tell us what you're interested in and consider it done. Things move along quickly here in basic and clinical research. I've dedicated myself to creating an optimal environment at the Institute for innovative research and surgery."

Rob was feeling more relaxed as he finished his drink and thought it might be the proper time to say hello from Dr. Ryan. "By the way, I was asked to pass along good wishes from an old friend."

"Oh?"

"Tom Ryan sends his best."

When he mentioned Ryan's name, Rob noticed Jamison's facial expression change. The smile, which greeted him earlier had transformed into a scowl.

After a pause, Jamison asked, "What did Tom have to say about me?"

Rob wasn't sure what to say. While Hal's words seemed congenial enough, his look and tone suggested something else. He wondered, *are Ryan and Jamison old friends or old enemies?*

"Tom mentioned that you once worked at the General. He told me you were a highly regarded surgeon as well as a brilliant researcher."

After a pause, Jamison responded with the pointed question, "Did Ryan tell you why I left Boston?"

"He mentioned something about a malpractice case."

Jamison could not contain his seething anger. His voice rose as he spoke, "Rob, I appreciate your candor. Honesty is something I value highly in relationships. But what you were told isn't exactly the way things happened, and you should know the truth."

He went on. "Back in the days when Ryan and I were a lot younger, both of us were full of energy and ambition. We wanted to give the world the benefits of everything transplant surgery had to offer. It's absolutely true that Tom and I were not just colleagues but friends, but then things changed. Ryan started going to cocktail parties with hospital bigwigs. He let his research and clinical responsibilities take a backseat. Appointed director of the Surgical Research Foundation he was handed purse strings to the big money flowing into the department. Eventually, he was also anointed department head by the hospital board."

Jamison went on. "Meanwhile, I was spending every wakeful hour in the operating room or over at the research building involved with my projects. Only two things mattered to me, taking good care of my patients and finding new ways to increase the success of transplant surgery. I became interested in stem cells and their capacity to influence rejection. That was nearly a decade ago, and few people were talking about how stem cells might be used in treatment.

I succeeded in cloning a line of amphibian stem cells that produced a special protein, which instruct recipient white cells to accept foreign tissue as its own. As long as I administered the stem-cell extract ahead of time I was able to prevent organ rejection in experimental animals."

"That's remarkable," Rob responded.

"Well, Rob," Jamison responded, "there's more to the story. It seems my hands were tied by Ryan, who wouldn't permit me to present any of the data."

"That's strange. Dr. Ryan is always pushing us to present our results at the transplant meetings. Why in the world would he stand in your way?"

"Ignorance and lack of foresight," Jamison shot back. "Ryan didn't stand up for me or my research when he needed to. Politics and money got in the way."

Rob was confused, he needed more details.

His host went on. "It had a lot to do with the lawsuit. I felt my research was at the point where we should start evaluating the stem-cell extract in patients. I designed a protocol and brought it to the human studies committee for review. While it appeared the committee members were quite impressed with the proposal, but when it came up for a vote it didn't pass. Ryan happened to be the committee's head. I was told that more extensive animal experiments were needed before proceeding on to humans. Later, one of the committee members confided in me that it was mainly Tom Ryan who put the kibosh on my project. Obviously, I was disappointed. The additional experiments would delay any opportunity of bringing the extract into clinical use by years. However, I had no choice but to comply with their wishes.

It was around that time that something I hadn't planned on happened, which changed everything. One of my patients, a man who had rejected two kidney transplants, was back and needing a third. I told him it wasn't going to be possible to do another transplant in view of the prior two rejections. He seemed to accept the situation, but a few days later I got a phone call from him. 'Dr. Jamison,' he said, 'I've decided not to continue dialysis and just let myself die.'"

Hal continued, "Perhaps my mistake was that I should have tried to get him committed to a psych ward, but I didn't. Instead, I gave him another option. It was unconventional, but could save his life. I decided to offer him the stem-cell extract, and he agreed."

"Jesus," Rob said.

"But, Rob, think about it for a moment. Major strides in medicine are often the result of a radical new approach to an old problem. Before my patient received the extract I had him sign a full set of the consent forms we usually use for clinical research, and he was aware of the risks involved, but before I went ahead there was one more thing I had to do." Jamison paused then continued. "I gave a dose of the extract to myself!"

Rob look at Jamison with amazement. "You're serious?"

"Yes, I wanted to make absolutely sure it wouldn't cause any serious side effects, so I tried it on myself, and there were none.

"Unfortunately, his operation didn't go so well. Postoperatively, he bled because of adhesions from his previous two surgeries. The complication had nothing at all to do with the extract. Tragically, he died on the third post-op day."

Rob listened as Jamison went on. "As if the loss of my patient wasn't enough, the real shock came when a subpoena arrived. It seems that without telling me, he'd shared the details of our private experiment with his wife. If he had lived, I'm sure she would have showered me with gratitude. Instead, the wife found a lawyer to sue me and Boston General. In spite of all the disclaimers signed indicating he was a willful participant, without official approval from the human studies committee, I became a vulnerable target. The hospital quickly settled the case for two million dollars, so it never made the newspapers.

"What really upset me more than anything was what, 'my friend', Tom Ryan did. He was mortified at the thought the government might step in and investigate infringement of the code on human experimentation then penalize the hospital by terminating all ongoing research grants. Ryan wasn't willing to take any chance on losing the money flowing into his coffers. Nothing about the potential value of my work mattered, nor the many years I had devoted to our transplant program. I was forced to submit my resignation, and I did."

Jamison drew in a breath as he finished his story then said, "Well, enough talk for now. Let's get everyone together and start dinner. I've given you more than enough to think about, and you must be famished."

Hal guided Rob toward the dining room where they met Pat and Sarah. Their dinner was about to begin. Although there were smiles on all the faces around the table, the conversation with Jamison had unsettled Rob. His mentor, Tom Ryan, had been portrayed in a less than favorable light, and that disturbed him.

The day that began early in Boston was nearly at its end on the west coast of Mexico. When they returned to their villa, all was quiet. The lights were off in Gloria's room just off the kitchen, and Josh was sleeping peacefully in his bed.

They entered their bedroom lit by a full moon on a cloudless night. Rob stepped behind Sarah as she began unzipping her dress. He kissed gently on the nape of her neck. In moments their clothes were off and strewn on the floor. Using whatever energy they had left, Rob and Sarah made love. Later, after she had fallen asleep, Rob got up, opened the doors to the balcony and stepped out. The night's cool breeze felt good. He saw the moon's reflection on the ocean and could hear the waves striking shore from where he stood. In the morning a visit to the Institute hospital awaited him.

12

Jorge arrived at the villa at 8 a.m. to pick Rob up and drive him to the Institute. The hospital stood amid a sculpted tropical setting that made it look more like a plush resort than a medical facility. When Rob was let off near the main entrance, he was met by Pat Hurley, who warmly greeted him.

"I hope you enjoyed our little dinner party last evening?"

"Oh, it was wonderful. Sarah and I really appreciated your hospitality."

"Did you find the villa acceptable?"

"It's more than acceptable. The place is fantastic."

"I'm so glad to hear that. Well, today, as outlined on your agenda, we'll begin with a tour of the Institute hospital." Pat led Rob inside the building.

The spacious lobby was adorned with paintings and sculptures. There were skylights everywhere. Rob was struck by the contrast with Boston General. When you walked into the lobby of the General, there was no doubt you were in a hospital. A phalanx of wheelchairs and oxygen tanks stood ready for use by the entry. Lines of ill-appearing patients were always present, either awaiting admission or discharge. He saw nothing like that at the Institute. It was easy to see how someone coming there for a transplant would feel comfortable.

As Pat made her way into the interior of the hospital, she began to talk. "You should note that our staff includes board-certified specialists in nearly every area: infectious disease, cardiology, nephrology, and pulmonary." She went on. "Our first floor has the operating rooms and surgical intensive care unit. Diagnostic radiology is also located on the first floor. The top two floors house the postoperative patients, each with a private room."

Rob asked, "Pat, can you give me an idea of how many transplant surgeries you do here?"

"On average we do four to six each day, which I'm sure you realize is more than most university hospitals back home."

"You're right," Rob said. "At most we only do three a day, and the General is one of the busiest transplant centers in the country."

As Rob walked the halls with Hurley, he couldn't help but be impressed by what he saw. She stopped in front of a large, glass-enclosed room that had a body scanner inside. "Rob, this is our Ultra-MRI. I'm not sure if you're familiar with this new prototype, but it represents a major advancement over the standard MRI scanners. Only a handful are up and running anywhere in the world. The Institute is fortunate to have the latest model."

"That's amazing," Rob said. "I never would've expected such technology in Mazatlan."

"Dr. Jamison has spared no expense to make the Institute one of the world's leaders in organ transplantation. Our biophysicists worked hard to make this Ultra do some pretty remarkable things. Its acquisition speed and spatial resolution have been increased to an unparalleled degree. This MRI can assess organ blood supply more accurately than a standard angiogram. It can pick up the smallest arterial branches without fail, and we've validated the results in dozens of patients. In fact, I can't recall the last time we did a conventional angiogram at the Institute."

Rob responded, "That's incredible."

As he stood there looking at the Institute's scanner he thought about Cheryl Jordan. *If only she'd been scanned with this Ultra, I would've known about her aberrant artery and never cut it.*

Hurley broke Rob's reflection. "Let's say we swing over to intensive care."

Pat led him over to the SICU. On entering, Rob noted the layout of their unit was practically identical to the General's. All the same state-of-the-art monitoring equipment was present. The only thing missing were the medical students and residents.

Passing by the central monitoring station, Pat introduced Rob to one of the physicians reviewing a chart. He was a pulmonary specialist, Dave Merwick.

"Hi, Dave," Pat said when he looked up from his chart. "If you're not terribly busy, could you spend a few minutes chatting with Rob Sanders? He's considering a position here as a transplant surgeon and came all the way from Boston General to visit us."

"Sure, Pat, I'd be happy to."

"Dave trained at Stanford before joining the Institute staff and has been a great help." After the introduction Pat left so they could talk.

Dave started. "Hey, those Red Sox of yours are something else. I always wanted to see a ballgame at Fenway, but haven't made it there yet. Anyway, it'd be great to have someone here from out east. We're kind of top-heavy on people who trained on the West Coast."

"Well, Dave, I hope I don't disappoint you, but I only did my transplant training in Boston. I was born in Chicago, and I did my residency at Northwestern. I'm actually a White Sox fan, but try to keep that fact quiet since I don't want to get lynched." Dave laughed.

"Chicago's good," Dave said. "When I was a resident I did a rotation at the University of Chicago. Had a great time for the two months I was in the city. Chicago has the best deep-dish pizza around, and the museums are phenomenal."

Rob asked Dave, "All kidding aside, could you give me your frank opinion on how things have been for you going for you here?"

"Well, I've been happy since the day I arrived. The lifestyle is fantastic. On my time off, I go sailing and play tennis. The weather is never bad. The hospital has all the best equipment and, better yet, there's no malpractice to worry about here in Mexico. This is as close to practice in heaven as you can get while still alive."

Pat returned and Rob prepared to leave. "Dave, thanks for your time. Hope talking with me didn't set your morning back too much."

"No sweat, Rob. Feel free to call me if you have any more questions, and good luck to you. I'll look forward to getting together if you decide to come aboard."

"Sure, I'd like that."

They shook hands, then Hurley and her guest proceeded down the hall.

"Pat, can I ask how long you've worked at the Institute?"

She smiled as she answered. "Since before it was built. I've been involved with the Institute from the time it was just an idea in Hal's head. At one time I was administrator for the Surgery Research Foundation at Boston General, and I worked directly under Tom Ryan. In fact, it was Ryan who introduced me to Hal." She paused briefly then went on. "I can recall the occasion like it was yesterday. Shortly after I started working at the General I had a meeting with Ryan in his office. We were discussing the details for an upcoming fundraiser when Hal just happened to stop by. Tom said, 'Pat Hurley, meet Hal Jamison. He's one of our top guns in organ transplantation and a damned good researcher. More important than that, he's a friend of mine!'"

Pat went on. "After Hal left Boston General, he offered me an opportunity to help him establish the Institute, and I decided to accept. Dr. Jamison is truly a visionary. All that you see before you is a result of his tireless efforts to create a unique, internationally recognized transplant center here in Mazatlan."

The news that Jamison and Hurley's relationship had its origin at Boston General made perfect sense to him. From what Rob had seen so far, their partnership had succeeded in achieving far more than he would ever have thought possible.

Their walk terminated directly in front of the doors leading to the operating rooms. "Rob, I'll drop you off here so you can change into scrubs and visit the operating rooms. For a surgeon like yourself, this is the place where you'll spend most of your day. I'm sure you're anxious to see what lies beyond."

She was absolutely right. While the rest of the hospital was indeed impressive, it was the operating rooms that were most critical to his work. Rob couldn't wait to go through the doors and see what was on the other side.

A moment later they opened, and a nurse motioned for Rob to enter. He took a step forward just inside the doors to meet the woman, who was dressed in surgical attire. She introduced herself as Sheila Morris, the coordinator for the operating rooms. Sheila walked him over to the men's changing area. He went inside and exchanged his street clothes for the Institute's blue scrubs. Donning the uniform of a surgeon, he felt back in his element. Perhaps he was three thousand miles from his hospital in Boston, but wearing those scrubs, he felt at home. Rob followed Sheila past several operating suites until they reached the room where Hal Jamison was scheduled to begin a kidney transplant. Hal was just outside the OR, scrubbing by the sink.

"Morning, Rob," Jamison said from behind his surgical mask. "Are things going well for you so far?"

"Yes," Rob answered. "Things couldn't be better."

"Glad to hear that. Now let me tell you something about our patient. He's Mr. Cheng, a fifty-two-year-old man who has been on dialysis for a couple of years and had enough. He came here from Hong Kong." Jamison went on. "The Cheng family is well known in Asia, where they own a large shipping firm. A good part of the trade flowing between mainland China and the rest of the world passes through the harbor in Hong Kong on Cheng-owned container ships.

"Mr. Cheng could have gone anywhere in the world for his surgery, but chose us. He actually told me that at University

Hospital in Beijing, he could have bought a new kidney for only $60 thousand US dollars.

"Organ transplant on the Chinese mainland has been a profitable business that brings in a considerable amount of hard foreign currency every year. Patients with money who need a transplant used to go there from other countries in Asia, Europe, or the Mideast. Now some, like Mr. Cheng, prefer to come here to Mazatlan instead."

Jamison finished scrubbing then entered the OR followed by Rob. Jamison introduced his assistant. "This is Don Adams. He's got the best set of surgical hands south of the border."

"Nice to meet you," Rob said acknowledging Jamison's helper."

Adams shot back, "I've heard a lot of good things about you." He continued, "I'm very much looking forward to working with you."

Jamison and Adams flew through the case as Sanders watched. Adams finished suturing the incision after Jamison left the patient's side. Hal took off his surgical gloves and motioned for Rob to follow him out of the OR.

"Come with me. Let's grab a cup of coffee." They left the operating room area and walked down a set of stairs to the cafeteria. Jamison picked up two apples from a basket and threw one to Rob. They made their way to the coffee station. With a fresh cup of coffee and apple in hand they sat at a quiet corner of the cafeteria to talk.

"I have one more case today, which you might find interesting," Jamison told Rob. "He's a twenty-two-year-old diabetic from Houston. His father is a prominent figure in the oil industry. Our patient has had diabetes since he was fourteen and has started to develop serious eye and kidney problems even though he's got the best diabetic specialists in Houston taking care of him."

Rob knew quite well what the next ten years would hold for the patient. He would likely need multiple laser treatments on his retinas to try and prevent blindness. Deterioration of his peripheral nerves would cause numbness in his feet and lower legs. Pressure ulcers could then occur, ultimately giving rise to infections. He would probably end up with amputation of toes that would gradually progress upward. His lower extremities would then gradually get whittled away until he was finally left with a pair of above-the-knee stumps. Kidney failure would eventually occur and require dialysis. Finally a heart attack or stroke would put an end to his unrelenting suffering.

Jamison went on. "While advances like the insulin pump have improved the outlook for severe diabetics, in reality it only serves to delay the inevitable." He continued, "Our patient has worn an insulin pump religiously for the last few years, and in spite of it his kidney function has continued to decline. Today, we'll give him a new pancreas and almost immediately his situation will improve. After a few days recovering, he will walk out of here freed from the ravages of diabetes.

"This case might be particularly interesting to you since I'll use a robot to do the operation."

Rob knew about robot surgery from journals, but no one in Boston had yet attempted to use the new technology.

Jamison explained, "Robotic surgery might take a bit longer, but the benefits to the patients are enormous. Its mechanical hands are only a fraction the size of an average human's and are guided with the aid of a sophisticated computer. The motion of my fingertips at the controls is converted to precise movements of the mechanical hands. The robot can cut, suture and do pretty much anything my own hands can do, only better." Jamison went on. "The smaller mechanical hands require only tiny incisions to permit entry. That leads to speedier recovery, smaller scars, and less blood loss." Jamison smiled as he finished talking.

Rob followed as Jamison bounded up the stairs to the operating rooms. Hal scrubbed and was once again ready for action. Both entered the OR together. The patient, Jonathan Oberman, was lying on the table under general anesthesia. He was connected to a ventilator that was breathing for him. Everything was ready for the operation to begin. The robot consisted of two parts. One was the unit that had a set of stainless steel mechanical arms and hands that would actually perform the surgery. The other was the control module. Its mechanical arms and hands looked like something that belonged on a General Motors assembly line.

Jamison took his seat at the control module and fit each of his fingers into their special receptacle on the control handles. The module was located about ten feet away from Jonathan's body and was connected by a single cord.

Don Adams, positioned the robot's hands just above the patient. Rob marveled as Jamison demonstrated how he could make the mechanical hands twirl around in any direction. No human hand was capable of making those moves.

Adams prepped the surgical field and made the initial two tiny incisions that would allow the robot's mechanical hands into the abdomen. At the controls, Jamison had a perfect close up view of the internal anatomy provided by a miniature fiber-optic lens connected to the robot's hand. Rob watched as the surgery took place ten feet from where they sat. Hal Jamison was playing the ultimate video game. The robotic hands he controlled were performing a complex operation that would make a huge difference in the life of the young diabetic lying on the table.

In diabetes, although the pancreas was unable to secrete enough insulin into the bloodstream that regulated glucose, it was still able to secrete important digestive enzymes into the small intestine. Therefore the old pancreas was left while the donor pancreas was placed at a different location, into the pelvis on top of the bladder. The new pancreatic duct was sown into the bladder so its digestive juices would pass harmlessly from the body in the urine. The blood supply to the new pancreas would come from connections made to an artery and vein in the pelvis just like with a kidney transplant.

Once connected to the pelvic vascular supply, the transplant would continuously produce enough insulin to keep the blood sugar level in the normal range. A diabetic patient with a pancreas transplant would be cured, and that was the intention for Jonathan Oberman.

Rob was in awe as he watched the small mechanical hands do the surgery. They were only one-half inch in width, whereas a normal human hand was three-and-a-half inches wide. The difference in the size of the incision required for a mechanical hand was nothing compared with the incision required to accommodate two human hands. Adams stood at the patient's side and his role was to feed suture material to the robot. In three hours, Jamison was finished with the operation and got up from his seat at the console while Adams closed the small surface incisions.

Rob was first to speak when they walked out the OR door. "That was one of the most amazing things I've ever seen. I had no idea robotic technology had advanced to this degree."

Jamison responded, "I dare say, Rob, if you hang around here a bit longer, you'd probably find a few more things that would amaze you."

Rob's day at the Institute hospital was nearing its end. His host looked tired, which was understandable after performing back-to-back transplants, one of which used robotics. As they started walking down the hallway toward the changing rooms, Jamison decided there was one more area he wanted to show his guest.

"Say, Rob, come with me. There's something else I want you to see." Jamison pivoted around and headed back down the hallway with his guest following close behind. He came to a door at the end of the corridor labeled "Organ Depository." With a swipe of his ID tag over the sensor at the entrance, the door opened and allowed them entry. Inside, the temperature plunged. In seconds Rob had goose bumps on his arms.

Jamison turned to Rob and said, "Don't worry, we won't be in here long enough to get frostbite." Hal turned on the light inside the darkened interior then walked to the center of the room, beckoning Rob to follow. Rob looked around. On shelves mounted to walls that surrounded them were dozens of tanks filled with a pinkish liquid. Bubbles of gas percolated upward from the base of each tank. For a moment it looked like he was in a refrigerated tropical fish store, only the tanks didn't contain fish. Instead, each had its own organ submerged. Jamison explained, "The organ depository is where we keep our harvested donor organs alive until we need them. A compound made from Coenzyme Q-10 helps keep them viable for extended periods of time. Co-Q 10 normally functions as a catalyst for cellular energy metabolism and as a free radical scavenger. With some alterations in its structure I found it could slow cell metabolism to a level seen in hibernating animals. The fluid in the tanks contains a concentration of the preservative delivered continuously to the organs via miniaturized pumps."

Jamison wanted Rob to know an additional fact. "You know, it's ironic. While I perfected the preservative methodology here, it was first conceived in my lab at Boston General."

Rob was floored by what he saw. "Dr. Jamison, when you say the organs can be kept alive for extended periods, exactly how long do you mean?"

"Back at the General you're used to implanting organs as soon as possible after removing them from a donor, preferably within hours. Here we can go weeks if necessary without loss of organ functionality. In the animal lab we've maintained organs for up to three months with no perceptible deterioration."

Rob responded, "That's incredible! I've never heard of anything comparable to that."

"Nor would I expect you to," Jamison answered then continued, "This organ bank is the result of years of dedicated research. No one anywhere else is close to duplicating our achievement."

"Well, you must be anxious to share your knowledge with the world. The Jamison Institute deserves special recognition from the medical community for such unprecedented work."

Hal smiled as he put his hand on Rob's shoulder, gently directing him back toward the entry to the frigid organ bank. Hal said,

"The world will find out everything in due time. The process of checking and double-checking all our data must continue before we make public the details of our research." Jamison continued, "Come, let's get out of here. I'm getting cold. Our technicians usually wear parkas in here." Jamison rubbed his upper arms to create warmth. He turned off the lights preparing to leave. When he opened the door, cold, moist air from inside created a mist of tiny ice crystals that penetrated a short distance into the hallway.

Jamison reminded Rob, "Tomorrow you'll visit our research building. In my opinion that's the crown jewel of the Institute. My colleague, Dr. George Fleming, will show you around, and we'll connect again toward the end of the day."

They shook hands before parting, but Jamison couldn't resist asking, "So, what do you think so far?"

Rob answered, "Wow! I've seen things today I never would've thought possible. My head is still spinning."

"Just wait till tomorrow."

When he exited the doors of the operating room area, Pat Hurley was waiting for him and walked him though one of the patient care floors.

Rob commented, "Pat, I don't see any isolation rooms."

Isolation rooms, were commonplace on standard transplant wards. When patients required high doses of agents to prevent rejection, their immune systems were so suppressed they became highly susceptible to infection. Special precautions were needed to prevent contact with infectious bacteria. Isolation rooms were sealed off from the hospital ventilation system and had their own separate air supply and exhaust. Anyone entering the room was required to put on a getup that looked like they were ready for a lunar landing, including facemask, head covering, gloves and gown.

Pat Hurley answered, "That's correct. You didn't see any isolation rooms because we don't have any. We have a totally different approach to immune suppression here, which you'll learn about shortly." As Rob continued walking toward the hospital entry, the significance of Pat's statement hit him. No isolation rooms and a totally different approach to immune suppression. He was intrigued.

"Goodbye, for now," Pat said, "I hope your tour has left you with a good impression."

Rob walked out of the hospital and saw Jorge waiting to pick him up. He took a deep breath and exhaled. Rob had seen things at the Institute he would have never expected to find at a hospital in Mazatlan. Yes, he was favorably impressed. What might lie ahead tomorrow in the research building was difficult to imagine. Rob slid onto the car's back seat as Jorge held the door open for him. Within minutes, he was back at his beachside villa.

13

It was late afternoon when Rob arrived. He found Gloria in the kitchen making preparations for dinner. She told him that Sarah and Josh had gone down to the beach, so he headed out to find them. He spotted Sarah lying on a blanket reading, while Josh sat nearby constructing a sand castle.

Rob took off his shoes and socks as he walked onto the sand. He wanted to surprise them, but Josh happened to turn his head. When he saw his father, Josh pointed at him and exclaimed, "Look, daddy's coming." He jumped up and started running toward him.

Rob dropped the shoes and scooped Josh up into his arms. Meanwhile, Sarah stood and approached him.

"How did it go?" she asked.

"The Institute hospital is an amazing place. I'll tell you all about it, but first, tell me what you did today."

Sarah gave Rob a rundown of her day's activities as they walked back to the villa.

"Pat Hurley connected me with one of the doctor's wives, Linda Merwick. Her husband is a pulmonary specialist at the Institute. She gave me a tour of the community, then we had lunch together in the city."

Rob cut in. "I met her husband, Dave, over at the hospital today. He seemed like a really friendly guy, trained at Stanford, says he loves working here and that the lifestyle can't be beat."

"Well, I saw the recreation center with Linda and the place is fantastic. They've got an Olympic-size swimming pool, half-a-dozen clay tennis courts, a running track, and an exercise area with every type of equipment known to man. There are classes in yoga, Tai Chi, spinning, and kickboxing. I felt like I was visiting a resort." Sarah went on. "After that I saw the school. It was far more advanced than anything I ever expected." She told Rob, "The kids start learning foreign language in preschool. They've got computers all over the place so the younger kids can begin learning how to use them early on.

"Linda even took me to do some food shopping at her favorite market. Later, we had lunch at a delightful restaurant near the waterfront. There were scores of interesting shops in the city center. That was my day in a nutshell."

They headed back to the city for and early dinner and chose a small restaurant that looked interesting. Both ordered lobster. After the server brought out the main course, Rob looked at his plate then stuck his fork in one of the small crustacean tails and held it up for Sarah. "They call these little things lobster?" He asked with a quizzical look.

Sarah had already taken a first taste. "They are definitely not the big New England ones we're used to but I have to admit it's pretty tasty."

As they ate, Rob told Sarah more about his tour at the hospital.

"I was in shock," Rob said to Sarah. "I couldn't believe the Institute has an MRI that makes the one we have at the General look antiquated, and the fact they're doing robotic surgery. It's something I might expect at Mayo or the Cleveland Clinic, but not here at a resort city in Mexico."

It was still light outside when they returned home and an idea popped into Rob's head. "Say, what if we all go for a swim?"

Sarah responded, "Sounds like a great idea."

Rob went upstairs to change. Sarah and Josh put on their swimsuits then headed for the pool.

Rob had been looking forward to the opportunity of getting Josh in the pool with him. His son had turned four, and it was time he learned how to handle himself in water. Rob gave Josh his first swimming lesson. They were all laughing, splashing, and having fun in the pool. For a moment Rob stopped swimming and stood still, thinking how nice it would be to have more time with his family if he took the job at the Institute.

Sarah threw a beach ball that hit him on the head while he wasn't looking. Rob turned toward Sarah as she laughed.

"I think it's time we head in. It's been a long day," she told him. "All right, if you insist," Rob said, reluctantly acquiescing to her suggestion. After drying off, the Sanders went inside to ready for bed.

14

Everyone except Gloria and Rob was still asleep when Jorge arrived at the beach villa in the early morning to pick him up. She had breakfast waiting for Rob when he came downstairs. He had never experienced service like that in his life. He gulped down some food, took a sip of his coffee, and ran out the door as he bid Gloria goodbye.

The research building was just up the road from the hospital. In between were villas where patients could recuperate after discharge before traveling back to their homes, which were usually abroad, at great distances from the Institute. The research facility itself was a three-story building similar in size to the hospital. Pat Hurley was waiting for Rob when he arrived. "Good morning, Rob. Hope you had a good night and are ready to see some more interesting things."

"Absolutely," Rob answered excitedly, pumped up for the day ahead.

"Let's go over to my office and chat for a moment before we proceed." Hurley walked with Rob past a security post and into the inner portion of the building. Her office was spacious and tastefully decorated. She invited him to take a seat.

"Rob, there's a small formality we must take care of before we tour. You must sign a confidentiality agreement before proceeding. Much of the work we do here is proprietary. We don't want anyone sharing information on the details of our research. I'm sure you can appreciate the situation."

Hurley pulled out the document for his signature. Rob glanced over the wording and put his signature at the bottom. With the agreement signed, she began his tour.

"At the Jamison Institute we're not interested in finding a better drug for high blood pressure or diabetes. Our focus is strictly on improving the ability to replace failing human organs." Pat explained, "Here, the goals are threefold. First, finding ways to prevent any deterioration of harvested donor organs awaiting transplant; second, to perform surgery with the lowest rate of complications; and third, to prevent transplant rejection through immune tolerance rather than immune suppression. Yesterday you already learned about the first two from Hal. Today, Dr. Fleming, our director of research, will fill you in on how we accomplish our third goal, immune tolerance."

They walked through the corridors of the research building and entered a room with a nuclear spectroscopic analyzer. Pat beamed as she proudly announced, "This is a one of a kind device. It can take a minute sample of any biological material and determine its precise chemical composition in a few minutes."

From there they walked into a laboratory area filled with rows of active bioreactor units. The spherical, stainless-steel containers held trillions of bacteria used to synthesize protein products using recombinant DNA technology.

Pat told Rob, "This is where we manufacture out biologically active proteins. Our factories are in each one of those metal spheres."

Rob wondered exactly what it was that they were 'cooking,' inside the bioreactors of the Jamison Institute.

They took the elevator to the third floor. When they got off, a locked security entrance confronted them. An identification biosensor was located at its side. Pat commented, "There are an awful lot of people who would love to know exactly what's going on behind this door."

Pat pressed her thumb against the identification panel. The door clicked open seconds later. When it shut behind them, Rob found himself in a different kind of place. The room was bathed in ultraviolet light, and his white shirt lit up. George Fleming, the chief scientist overseeing the research facility, was standing directly in front of them.

"George, this is Rob Sanders from Boston General. He's looking at a position doing transplants at the hospital. Fleming addressed Rob with his prominent British accent. "Dr. Sanders, what a pleasure. I've heard so many good things about you." He shook his guest's hand, handed him a protective cover for his clothing, and told him, "Here, you'll need to slip this on before we proceed."

Pat spoke up. "I'll leave the two of you to look around the rest of the research building on your own. That way you can use your scientific jargon with each other and not make me feel bad because I don't understand a word of it. Have fun, gentlemen." With that said, Pat turned and walked out the door.

"In case you're wondering," Fleming said to Rob, "this room is bathed in UV light to kill airborne bacteria and virus. We need to minimize unwanted contamination entering the research space. Please try to avoid looking directly at the light sources, so you don't burn your retina."

Fleming led Rob out of the decontamination area and into one of the adjacent labs. Before he said anything that might divulge secrets of the Institute, Fleming asked, "Dr. Sanders, have you signed a confidentiality agreement?" Rob nodded and told him, "Yes, I went over that issue with Pat before starting the tour."

Fleming responded, "Very well then, we can continue." They entered a lab that had racks holding a multitude of glass flasks. Each flask had a bluish fluid at its bottom. The overhead lighting was dimmed.

"This is where we maintain our amphibian stem-cell lines in culture." Fleming went on. "The cells happen to be exquisitely sensitive to their ambient environment. To thrive, they require precise control of temperature, lighting, and nutrition.

"The cells in these flasks produce the immune tolerance protein discovered by Dr. Jamison when he was at Boston General. I received my doctorate in biochemistry from Oxford and did postdoctoral work at MIT. My proteomics lab there was just a stone's toss across the Charles River from the General. It seems like eons ago that Hal and I met. That's when he first told me about the stem-cell extract, which could prevent rejection. Collaborating with him I managed to purify the active substance in his extract, a 180-amino-acid-long protein. I worked out its three-dimensional structure and later identified the sites on the protein responsible for its biological effect."

Fleming explained, "The process of purifying the protein directly from salamander stem cell cultures is quite tedious and yields only small quantities. After a lot of effort, we succeeded in splicing the gene that governs its synthesis into a strain of *E. coli*. Presently, our bioreactors are producing the protein. Recombinant DNA technology will allow us to make as much as we want. I suppose we could even crank up production so that in a couple of weeks we would have enough to fill a swimming pool, enough to supply the whole world!"

Indeed, George Fleming had worked long and hard on the stem-cell protein. His research so consumed him he would dream about the details of three-dimensional structure the way other men dream about the contour of a woman's body. George knew precisely how it was able to bind white-cell receptors and inhibit the cellular responses resulting in immune tolerance. He knew the object of his study so well, he could write the protein's entire amino-acid sequence from memory.

Fleming went on. "While we plan to keep the stem-cell line alive for backup, all production in the future will come directly from the *E. coli*. This Institute owes a lot to the stem cells' unique protein. It helped give us the outstanding clinical results we have by preventing rejection reactions. The protein has opened a whole new range of possibilities for the scores of sick people who come here for their transplants. Eventually, it'll do the same for countless others around the world in need of a new organ!"

"Do you mean you're actually giving the protein to transplant patients here at the Institute?"

"We most certainly do. Every one of our cases receives an infusion containing the stem-cell protein prior to undergoing their transplant. Once it's given, the patient's white cells will recognize the tissue antigens of the transplant as their body's own. Because of this amazing protein, we don't need to treat our patients with immunosuppressive drugs and consequently no increased susceptibility to infection or cancer."

Rob was stunned by Fleming's revelation. Now he understood why on his tour of the hospital there were no isolation beds. Giving the stem-cell protein was the Institute's "different approach" to dealing with rejection Pat Hurley alluded to.

Fleming escorted Rob over to the elevator. "Let's go down to the second floor," he suggested. "That's where our animal labs are located." Fleming used his thumbprint to gain entrance to the second floor through a security door just as Pat had. Once inside, they were greeted to a chorus of howling monkeys. George led the way into a room where two lab technicians were performing a procedure on one of the animals lying on an operating table in the center of the room. Cages of other primates at various stages of recuperation from surgical procedures surrounded the room.

Fleming walked over to one of them. Rob saw the healed scar from an operation on the animal's lower abdomen. "In this cage," Fleming told him, "our primate subject received a kidney transplant four weeks ago from an unmatched donor. The ape received an infusion of stem-cell protein several hours prior to the transplant. So far there are no signs of rejecting the kidney." Fleming added, "Perhaps that doesn't sound so dramatic based on what you've heard about the immune tolerance protein, but there is one critical difference to this animal's transplant. It didn't come from another ape. It's a xenograft...it came from a human cadaver."

Rob's jaw dropped as Fleming's words registered in his brain. He realized the work being done at the Institute went well beyond the simple resurrection of Jamison's research at the General. It was blazing a new trail that would forever change the way medicine was practiced.

Xenografts, transplants from one species into another, typically produced a fulminating rejection reaction within hours of implant. A decade earlier surgeons tried to transplant the heart of a baboon into a newborn nicknamed "Baby Fae." The infant was suffering from a rare congenital heart disease. Her underdeveloped heart couldn't supply her tiny body with the necessary blood, and she was destined to die. The surgeons theorized that the newborn's immune system was so young it wouldn't recognize the baboon heart antigens as foreign and therefore tolerate the transplant. Unfortunately, the primate heart worked well for only a day. Then a rejection reaction began and, sadly, the infant died a short time later. The unsuccessful experience with Baby Fae put an end to any future attempts to use xenografts in humans.

Rob had seen for himself that successful transspecies organ transplantation was possible, and he fully understood the implications. The perennial limitation to transplantation surgery was the shortage of available organs. The list of people waiting for a transplant was already long and getting longer. Rob was staring at a possible solution to the problem of limited organ supply inside the cage in front of him. *If a human kidney could be successfully transplanted into a primate, then a primate kidney could be transplanted into a human using the same approach!*

There might be no future need for registry lists, no need for prolonged suffering with poorly functioning organs, and definitely no need to die waiting for a compatible organ donor. As he stood there in front of the cage with the monkey harboring a human kidney, Rob had a vision of what the future might hold.

As his tour was ending, Fleming was about to say goodbye to Rob and let him take the elevator down to the first floor. As Rob shook hands with Fleming, he told him, "I want to thank you for showing me around the research building. After what I've seen here today, there's no doubt in my mind you and Dr. Jamison will revolutionize the way we do transplantation. Both of you deserve to be properly acknowledged."

"All in due time, Dr. Sanders, all in due time, but I'm pleased you acknowledge the magnitude of our achievement."

The doors to the elevator closed and silence surrounded him. However, Rob's brain was reeling. He tried to digest the startling things seen on his tour. When the elevator opened, he walked toward the entrance of the building deep in thought. Pat Hurley was waiting for him by the exit, and Rob might have walked right past her had she not moved in front of him, nearly blocking his path.

"Well, Rob, how'd things go on the tour with Fleming?"

"To be honest, I've seen some truly remarkable things here. Things I would never have thought possible."

"Rob, I'm sure you can now understand why I had you sign that confidentiality document. There are many who would pay a king's ransom to know exactly what we're doing in our research labs. To make sure that we successfully complete our projects and provide the great benefit to our patients, we must keep the details of this work top secret, at least for now. Only a select few from outside the immediate Institute family have been privileged to learn about our research activities."

Pat looked down at her watch to check the time. "Well, Rob, it's still early, and the rest of this glorious day is yours to enjoy. Tomorrow you have a breakfast meeting with Dr. Jamison at his home. After that you'll be free again until your flight back to Boston at 5 p.m.

"Perhaps I won't see you again, if you choose not to accept the job offer, but in any event I'd like you to know it's been a real pleasure meeting you and your lovely wife. I wish you luck whatever your final decision may be." Pat graciously extended her hand and warmly shook Rob's.

With that, she turned and walked back into the interior of the research facility. As he left the building, Rob was still thinking about the wonders within its unpretentious walls. It could make organs available to thousands in need of a transplant around the world.

Rob made his decision regarding the job. No other program gave a comparable opportunity to access the world's most advanced surgical technology and research. All that, coupled with an outrageous salary and fantastic lifestyle—it was an offer he couldn't possibly say no to. Rob was prepared to accept the position at the Institute.

After giving the tour, Fleming went back to his office and began reviewing production schedules for the latest batch of bio-engineered Chimera Factor protein.

Fleming had shown Rob a lot of interesting things in the research building, but not everything. As they had walked the corridors, he purposely avoided entering Jamison's private lab. Only he, Adams, and Jamison himself ever went inside.

Jamison nicknamed his lab the "pet shop," referring to the unique surgical creations residing inside. His special pets were held in reserve for the CEOs of pharmaceutical companies who required further convincing of the Chimera Factor's true power. It was one thing to read through a file of data that indicated a transplanted organ was free of rejection. It was an entirely different thing to gaze upon living animals whose bizarre construction could only have been made possible by achieving perfect immune tolerance. If it would help seal a lucrative deal with one of the companies bidding for the rights to the Chimera protein, they would invite its CEO to visit the pet shop.

As he sat at his desk, George thought for a moment about Sanders. *Seems like a nice guy, and he's got to be a good surgeon if*

Jamison wants him so badly. I just hope he can handle the work here. We don't need another Wes O'Brien.

There was once a time when George Fleming was driven by his love of science and a desire to use his talent to help humanity, but that was ancient history. The only thing that motivated Fleming now was his love of money. He would make sure the Institute got the best offer from its pharmaceutical company suitors for the Chimera Factor. His share of the prize would probably be enough to make him the wealthiest PhD on the planet.

15

Rob awoke early and couldn't go back to sleep. He took a walk on the beach as the sun was rising then swam laps in the pool. At 9 a.m. he drove the Land Rover to Jamison's estate for his breakfast meeting. The drive didn't take more than a few minutes. Rob stopped at the front gate and pressed the buzzer announcing his arrival. A security camera looked on as the gates were opened. Once again Rob rode up the drive lined by royal palms that led to Jamison's mansion.

Rob had been on track to accept the job offer from the Cleveland Clinic. He came to Mazatlan for what he thought would be nothing more than a free vacation with his family. Now Rob was thinking in earnest that his future might be at the Jamison Institute.

A servant met him at the entry and led him along the path through the garden alcove to the house. Once inside he was shown down a hallway to Jamison's study. Hal was sitting at a worktable at the far side of the room. He held a surgical hemostat in his hands and was wearing a pair of magnification lenses, the kind usually worn in the OR while performing a delicate surgical procedure. "Excuse me, Dr. Jamison," the housekeeper said, interrupting his concentration, "your guest is here."

Jamison straightened up, his eyes peering over the top of the spectacles.

"Ah, Rob. Welcome, welcome. Why don't you come on over here? Let me show you something interesting." Rob stepped up to the worktable. Set before Jamison was an array of surgical instruments—forceps, scissors, scalpel and suture, but it wasn't an operation he was performing. Instead, he was constructing fishing flies. A variety of hooks, feathers, and shards of animal fur also lay on the table.

"Just a little hobby of mine," Hal said and added, "You might have guessed, I like fly-fishing."

Looking at the assortment of feathers on the worktable, Rob recognized their vivid colors. They came from the birds living within the mansion's garden alcove.

Hal explained that flies were constructed to resemble the size and color of insects that river fish favored in their diet. From what Rob saw, Jamison took the same meticulous care to construct his lures as he did in the operating room. Rather than using store-bought line to make his flies, he used delicate but strong surgical suture. Rob spotted open packets of 7-0 Ethicon, a fine synthetic nylon typically used for operations like vascular repair or plastic surgery.

Jamison held up one of his creations in a forceps and invited Rob to take a closer look at it through a magnifying glass.

"A fish fly," Jamison explained, "has several components, just like a body of the insect." He used the tip of a pen to point out the parts of the lure.

"The wings and tail are made of feather, but the body is from the fur of a white-tailed deer. It's all bound together around the base of a hook by nylon suture."

As Rob looked around the room, he saw evidence of his host's success as an outdoorsman. Jamison identified the fish mounted on the walls as species of cutthroat, rainbow, and brown trout. They appeared so real, it seemed like they were swimming in a school.

"Don't get the wrong idea," Hal told Rob, "I usually catch and release. It's only rarely I bring one home." Jamison added, "Unfortunately, there's no trout in the rivers down here. For fly-fishing I head north to my ranch at Jackson Hole. I brought the trophies on the wall down here to remind me of the place I really love."

Conspicuously absent from the wall were any marlin, bonita, or dolphin, for which the waters off Mazatlan were well known to sport fishermen. Hal told Rob, "I have no interest in deep-sea fishing. I can't see myself smoking a cigar, drinking beer, and inhaling diesel fumes while sitting at the stern of some boat. Imagine the boredom of being strapped into a chair for hours on end while the boat goes trolling around looking for a fish to take the hook. That's definitely not for me. What I like is standing knee deep in a cold river current and casting for my prize."

Jamison walked over to the opposite side of the study where the hunting prizes were located. He pointed out the mounted heads of a white-tailed deer, elk, and bighorn mountain goat. Near the room's entry, a crossbow hung on the wall. Jamison saw that Rob's attention was drawn to it.

"Oh, that," Jamison said to him. "It's a gift from a grateful patient whose hobby is woodworking. He knew I like to hunt and handmade the crossbow for me."

Jamison lifted the bow, which had an arrow in place, from its wall mount and handed it to Rob. "He did a hell of a good job, don't you think?" When Rob hesitated to take the weapon, Jamison added, "Oh, don't worry, the safety is on. It won't go off."

Rob held the crossbow and looked over its exquisite hand carving. Jamison went on. "When I hunt I prefer using a crossbow. I never liked guns. They're not enough challenge. With a rifle and scope you can shoot a buck from hundreds of yards away with no effort. Taking a twelve-point buck down with an arrow from thirty yards off, now that's real sport."

A large oil painting with a panoramic view of mountains rising steeply above a plain and a river winding through the foreground was mounted above the fireplace. "Nice painting," Rob said. "Looks familiar, but I just can't place it."

Hal responded, "The Tetons in Wyoming, with the Snake River in the foreground. You know, Rob, I believe every man should have a passion for something other than his profession. Well, mine is fly-fishing. Do you like the outdoors?"

"Sure. But I've never had a chance to do anything like fly-fishing," Rob answered.

"Maybe one day you'll join me at my place up north. I think you'd enjoy yourself. Fly-fishing is a completely unique experience from anything you've done before. But, let me warn you, you might become as addicted as I am." Jamison continued. "Some years back I was fortunate enough to pick up a parcel of land right on the banks of the Snake." Jamison motioned toward the painting. "In fact, my place is just around that bend of the river you see in the picture. One of the fringe benefits of owning a jet is that I can go to Jackson Hole on short notice, if I manage to finagle a little time off."

Rob noticed an unusual bronze statue on Jamison's desk. "What's that?" he asked.

"Ah, that's a Chimera, a mythical creature that had the body parts of different animals. As you can see, it has the head and body of a lion, but its tail is a snake. A goat's head protrudes from its back. According to ancient Greek legend, the Chimera breathed fire and terrorized local villagers.

"In fact, we borrowed the Chimera's name for our stem-cell protein. It made perfect sense since harboring an organ that was once a part of another animal creates a biological Chimera. What better title for an immune tolerance protein that makes such transplants possible?" Jamison changed the topic. "You must be getting hungry. What about some breakfast?"

As they walked to the kitchen, Jamison broached the question he was waiting to ask, "So, now that you've had a chance to see our hospital and research facility, what did you think?"

"Frankly, I'm still in a state of shock. The Institute is truly remarkable. What we're doing at Boston General is important, but it doesn't approach the level of what's been accomplished here. Your work in organ preservation and immune tolerance is light-years ahead of ours."

"I'm glad to hear we made a favorable impression, and I hope you're seriously considering joining us. Personally, Rob, I don't think there is a program anywhere else in the world that could offer you the opportunities you would have here."

"Dr. Jamison, the more I see, the more I agree with you."

Rob and Jamison sat at the table. They had fresh-squeezed orange juice, coffee, and egg white omelets prepared by the cook.

"Are there any questions I can answer before you head back to Boston?"

Rob thought for a moment and answered, "I can't get over the immune tolerance action of the amphibian stem-cell protein. How in the world did you ever figure that out?"

Jamison cleared his throat. "You know, it's a funny story that dates all the way back to when I was a kid growing up in Minnesota. I used to go scrounging about in the local marshes and had a terrarium filled with the captives of my adventures—a few frogs, some turtles, and a blue-spotted salamander.

"One day a turtle latched onto the tail of the little amphibian and wouldn't let go. A minute later its tail fell off, and I was horrified. My mutilated salamander slithered away under some rocks in the tank. In a few days it reappeared, and miraculously the amputated tail had almost completely grown back!

"That observation as a child became a source of unending interest for me. At the General I did a series of experiments, which indicated that limb amputation in salamanders caused stem cells to rapidly multiply and differentiate into mature components. Eventually, the entire amputated limb was reformed. I isolated some of those stem cells and grew them in tissue culture.

"Something told me that if I continued studying them, the lowly amphibian's stem cells would yield something of real importance to humans. About a year later, and quite by accident, they did."

Rob was totally caught up in Hal's story, barely picking at his breakfast.

Jamison went on. "In experiments, I amputated salamander limbs, then surgically reconnected them to examine their viability. But then I made an error.

"To speed the project along, I was working on two of the salamanders at once. I surgically removed their right forelimbs and stored them overnight. The next day I reconnected them.

"By mistake I switched the forearms onto the wrong animals. The real shock came when the rejection reaction I anticipated never happened. Imagine for a moment taking the arm of a human cadaver and implanting it onto another person. To avoid rejection, you'd need to give the recipient massive doses of immunosuppressive drugs. In the case of the salamanders, no such drugs were administered. I reasoned the stem cells somehow played a role in mediating the immune tolerance for the accidental limb transplants. I went back to the stem-cell cultures and prepared an extract. When I administered the extract to a rabbit given an incompatible donor kidney, there was no rejection! Something in the extract was clearly able to induce immune tolerance.

"It didn't take long to realize the tremendous tool I had uncovered and its potential in human transplantation. The protein we now know as the Chimera Factor was ultimately isolated and analyzed by Dr. Fleming. It induces such perfect immune tolerance we no longer have to use standard immunosuppressive drugs."

"I must say, Dr. Jamison, that's quite a story. You should be congratulated on your discovery and your persistence." Rob asked, "I can understand stem cells differentiating to form new tissue, but why should they produce anything like the Chimera protein that works on the immune system?"

"That's an excellent question, and I'll give you my theory. It's known that regenerating cells express fetal antigens on their surface. That could set up a situation where healing injured tissue might be recognized as foreign by the organism's white cells that lost the ability to remember those fetal antigens. A deadly rejection reaction might then occur, destroying the new tissue. By producing the Chimera protein, the stem cells help prevent that self-destructive reaction."

"Sounds reasonable," Rob said, nodding in affirmation.

Jamison continued, "In other experiments I found out that timing is crucial. The Chimera protein must be administered within a window of hours prior to exposure to a new donor organ otherwise the typical rejection reaction will ensue."

Rob looked down at his barely touched breakfast. As he listened to Jamison speak about Chimera Factor, he came to understand the basis of the Institute's success. Perhaps there was some luck involved in discovering the immune tolerance protein. If Jamison hadn't made the mistake of switching salamander limbs, the Chimera protein might still be unknown. However, the breakthrough only took place because Jamison put all the pieces of the puzzle together and did so brilliantly. There was no doubt in Rob's mind. Hal Jamison was a true genius.

16

After their meeting, Hal walked Rob out to the Land Rover. As Jamison said goodbye, he once again encouraged him to consider his offer to work at the Institute. Rob drove back to the beach villa. The rest of the day was his until the late afternoon when they had to get ready for the flight back to Boston.

Rob returned to find Sarah and Josh in the pool. When Josh saw his father approaching, he climbed out of the pool and exclaimed, "Daddy, look!" He jumped feet-first into the water. Josh held his breath and dog-paddled into his waiting mother's arms. Rob laughed and clapped his hands for his son's success.

The time spent in Mazatlan had been thoroughly enjoyable. The sad fact was that it would soon be ending. Rob realized that tomorrow he would be back to work at Boston General. Not wasting any time, he ran upstairs, changed into his swimsuit, then hurried back to join his family in the pool.

Gloria served them lunch on the patio. Afterward they drove into town and shopped for souvenirs. They bought a Mexican shirt for Rob, a toy donkey and sombrero for Josh, and a decorative handmade, silver-plated mirror for Sarah.

After returning, it didn't take long for them to pack. With suitcases filled, they prepared to bid Gloria farewell. Josh started sobbing and asked his mother if Gloria could come back home with them. In a gentle voice, Sarah explained that Gloria's home was in Mexico and that someday they could go back to visit her.

Jorge arrived in the Mercedes to drive them to the airport. Rob thanked Gloria for all she had done then took out his wallet.

Gloria held up her hand in protest. "No, Dr. Rob, that is not necessary. I have already been paid for my work, and it was a pleasure to be with you and your family. Josh is such a wonderful little boy." Rob hugged her and got into the car.

The jet with the logo of the Jamison Institute on its side was on the tarmac awaiting them. Jorge pulled the car up to the jet, and the flight attendant ushered the occupants onto the aircraft. Once the door was secured, the attendant came over to their seats. She held out a manila envelope for Rob to take.

"Dr. Sanders, I was asked to give this to you." The jet taxied down the runway and a minute later was up in the air. Josh had his face pushed against the window looking at the view of the city and its bay from the sky. Rob and Sarah's eyes met, and they smiled contentedly to each other. The vacation had been good for all of them.

After getting settled, Rob opened the envelope and began to read the letter inside:

Dear Dr. Sanders,

It was a pleasure meeting you and your wife. I hope your visit to the Institute was enjoyable and informative. Once more, I'd like to remind you of our confidentiality agreement.

You left a favorable impression on Dr. Jamison. He sincerely believes that you would be an outstanding addition to our program. In light of that, he has instructed me to tell you that should you elect to join our staff, as a special signing bonus, the deed of ownership to the beach villa and Land Rover will be transferred to your name. The previous terms for salary and benefits otherwise remain unchanged.

Have a safe trip back to Boston.

Pat Hurley, Administrator, Jamison Institute

Rob handed the letter to Sarah, who read it intently, her eyes growing wider as she proceeded down the page. When Sarah finished, she looked over at Rob and asked, "Am I dreaming? My God, Rob, this is unbelievable!" Sarah gave him an enormous hug.

Rob told her, "It seems too good to be true, but it's here in writing. They're giving me the opportunity to do state-of-the-art transplant surgery with an incredible salary. We even get a house and car as part of the deal!" Rob paused to take in a breath then continued, "It's an offer I can't refuse."

When the limousine dropped them off at their apartment back in Boston, it was after 2 a.m. Rob carried his sleeping son inside and put him to bed. Sarah and Rob were exhausted, but instead of going directly to bed, they walked over to his desk. Rob picked up the Jamison Institute contract. He took a pen and signed his name then sealed it in the FedEx packet as Sarah looked on. First thing in the morning, after Rob headed back to the hospital, she would call FedEx. It was entirely possible that by the end of the day that had already begun, his signed contract would be in Pat Hurley's hands.

17

At 6:30 a.m. Rob was in the SICU at Boston General for morning report. His time off in Mexico had been great, but he was ready to once again immerse himself in doing surgery. One thing left him feeling uneasy on his return—how would he tell Dr. Ryan about his decision to take a job at the Jamison Institute?

Rob learned from Jason that during his vacation, Fitch Jr. had been discharged home. His father was still in the hospital undergoing the final days of immunosuppressive treatment to prevent rejection of the liver segment his son had given him. Later, when the team stopped by to round on Mr. Fitch Sr., Rob saw him for the first time with a normal complexion. His yellowish-brown skin color was gone. He looked more energetic, even though his transplant was only one week before. Rob reviewed the most current lab values, all of which indicated Fitch's new liver was working fine.

Cheryl Jordan would be going home in the next day or two. She was still in isolation completing her round of immunosuppressive drug treatment. When Rob entered her room, she was out of bed and sitting in a chair. Fortunately, no infectious complications had occurred while he was away. Rob was dressed in protective garb, including special coveralls, a surgical mask and gloves to prevent direct contact. However, when Cheryl saw Rob come into her room, she got up from her seat and gave him a hug before he could stop her.

"Hey, hold on a minute," Rob said as he pulled back. "I'm glad to see you're doing well, but let's try to avoid getting too close while you're still on high doses of immune suppressive drugs."

"Oops. Sorry, Dr. Sanders," Cheryl said, "but I was so glad to see you back, I couldn't help myself."

That afternoon, Rob assisted Bill Mayer in doing a pancreas transplant. Mayer knew that Rob's trip to Mexico was more than a vacation. Virginia Wheeler let him know he was also going there for a job interview. After their case finished, Rob sat with Mayer in the surgical lounge, each with a cup of coffee in their hand.

"I heard you went down to Mexico to check out a job," Mayer said, getting directly to the point.

"Yes, I visited a place called the Jamison Institute."

"So, how'd it go?"

"Well, I found it a surprisingly sophisticated facility in nearly every respect. For example, they've been doing robotic transplant surgery for quite some time, and the research they're doing is phenomenal. Overall, I have to say, I was quite impressed." Rob was careful not to give out any details that might jeopardize his confidentiality agreement.

"Are they getting good results with their transplants?" Mayer asked.

"Well, I understood their record of success is at least comparable to any university program and probably better than most."

Mayer told Rob, "I didn't know there were any transplant programs in Mexico. In spite of the major medical centers such as Guadalajara or Mexico City, I was under the impression patients from there traveled to the US for their transplants."

Mayer went on. "You aren't seriously thinking of taking the job there? Are you?"

"Well, I'm giving the Institute serious consideration but haven't made my mind up as yet. A lot of things are factoring into the decision."

"Rob, it's no secret I'd love to have you stay on here. I even think I could get Ryan to sweeten his offer by a few thousand dollars."

"Thanks, Dr. Mayer, I appreciate that."

There was no way Rob could tell Mayer the truth. Not only had he already made up his mind, but he had signed a contract. It was only right that he first break the news to his chief, Dr. Ryan.

The next morning while making rounds, Rob received a page from Virginia who inquired, "Hope you had a good trip."

"I had a great time," Rob answered. "The weather was terrific."

"Rob, Dr. Ryan would like you to see him today at 3 p.m., if your schedule permits."

"Sure, it shouldn't be a problem. I was meaning to call you and set up an appointment anyway. I'll stop by at three."

Just before the meeting, Rob took an elevator to the eighth floor where the administrative offices were located. He walked into the chairman's office and greeted the secretary.

"Hey, Virginia, how are you?"

"Very well, thank you." She saw his tan and commented, "Say, it looks like you got some color while you were on that job interview of yours." Virginia smiled and went on. "I'll let Dr. Ryan know you're here. He's expecting you." She buzzed her boss on the intercom and announced Rob had arrived. As he walked in to see the chief, his palms were sweaty.

"Come on in, Rob, and have a seat. Hope you had a nice trip to Mexico. Did Sarah and Josh enjoy themselves?"

"Yes. They had a great time," Rob said. "The trip went much better than I expected. He hesitated briefly before continuing. "To be honest, sir, I saw some things there that were truly astounding."

"Such as?"

"Well, you might find this hard to believe, but they've been using robotics to do many of their operations. The surgery takes a bit longer and is more challenging from a technical standpoint, but results in less blood loss and tissue injury, allowing for a speedier recovery."

Ryan responded, "I've known about the robotic technique for some time. It was first used in heart surgery, mainly for valve repair and occasionally for coronary bypass. Now its role is expanding into noncardiac surgery. It makes sense that it could be applied to transplants as well. Let me share this with you, Rob. I've submitted a proposal for a new robotic device on our next budget. I think I'm on solid ground saying the odds that the hospital board will approve it are good."

"That's fantastic, Dr. Ryan."

"There's another thing I'd like to tell to you about, Rob. I was able to come up with some additional funding for your position if you decide to stay. I wanted you to know we can go up on the offer by fifteen-thousand dollars."

Rob didn't know if his face expressed the turmoil he felt inside. It was an honor to be considered for a position at Boston General and work as the colleague to a man of Ryan's stature. He wanted to say, *Yes, I'll stay,* but he couldn't.

"Chief, I feel privileged by your offer, but after thinking long and hard on our options, Sarah and I have decided to take one of the other opportunities." Rob swallowed hard then continued, "I've signed a contract with the Jamison Institute."

Ryan's expression took on a look of disbelief. After a pause he spoke, "Well, I wouldn't be telling you the truth if I didn't say I'm disappointed. Many of us in the department were hoping you'd stay on as junior attending, but you obviously have made a commitment elsewhere. That being the case let me be the first to congratulate you. Perhaps I can take some consolation knowing that wherever you go, and whatever you do, the high standards of Boston General will follow you."

"Of course, Dr. Ryan, that goes without saying."

"And Rob, please keep in touch with us. After all, we consider you one of our family."

Rob was touched by the sincerity of Ryan's words. He knew he would miss the people and the institution, but it was time to move on.

Their meeting coming to an end, Rob stood. "Thanks again, Dr. Ryan, for your generous offer. It means a lot to me to be held in such high regard by you. I only hope I've made the right decision."

"You're an outstanding young physician," Ryan told him. "In the future many of the decisions you need to make will be difficult. Listen to what your gut tells you and never second-guess yourself. Don't look back. That's the best advice I can give you."

Rob was about to leave when Ryan stopped him.

"Oh, Rob, before I forget." He reached into a drawer of his desk, pulled out a small wooden box and handed it to Rob. "Please accept this small gift from the department." Rob had no idea what it was. He opened the box and inside was a set of surgical magnifying lenses. The Zeiss glasses were worth a small fortune. Rob had to hold back tears, and his voice choked as he told his chief, "I don't know what to say. I've learned so much here at the General. I can't possibly express my gratitude in words." Then, carrying his coveted gift, Rob left Ryan's office to do his next case in the operating room. He needed more time to digest the meeting that had just concluded. One thing was for sure, he was going to the Jamison Institute to start his practice in transplant surgery. There was no turning back.

18

It wasn't difficult for Rob and Sarah to up anchor and leave Boston. The three years they had lived there were good, but they had no family roots to tie them to the region, and Josh was still too young for changing schools to be an issue. They had enjoyed living amid such a vibrant historical city, but now it was time to move on.

They passed along their used furniture to several needy families living in the apartment complex. The van sold two days after Rob put a sign up in the hospital cafeteria. The only things they would take to Mexico were loaded into several suitcases. The exception was Rob's library of medical textbooks. They were crated for shipment and would probably arrive a few weeks after he did.

When their jet landed at the Institute airfield they stepped off the plane greeted by a balmy breeze. Jorge's car was waiting on the tarmac. He approached them waving and smiling. "Welcome back to Mazatlan." Reaching out to take Rob's briefcase and Sarah's carry-on he asked politely, "May I?"

Rob noticed a small plane on the other side of the runway. A gray van was parked next to it, and a red Porsche with its convertible top down stood alongside the van. A man appeared to be in the process of unloading some items from the plane into the back of the van while another stood next to the Porsche and was talking on a cellphone. Rob couldn't quite make out their faces. The man loading the van closed its rear door and drove off. Then the one with the cellphone got into the car. Rob heard the screech from the wheels of the Porsche and watched the driver wave to Jorge as he sped by them.

Once they were settled into Jorge's Mercedes, Rob asked, "Jorge, did you know the man driving the Porsche?"

"Oh, that was the pilot of the plane across the way. His name is Ricardo Pedraza, but everyone calls him Dr. Ricky."

"He's a doctor?"

"Oh yes, and he's also a very good pilot. It's said that he learned how to fly when he was so young he had to sit on his father's lap to reach the controls." Jorge continued, "But I'm surprised you don't already know Dr. Ricky, since he is a surgeon at the Institute."

Rob thought for a minute and told Jorge, "I don't recall seeing him on my previous visit. Maybe I'll meet him at the hospital tomorrow."

"Yes, I'm sure you will," Jorge responded.

Their car pulled up at the beach villa where they were treated to Gloria's welcoming smile. Josh ran forward as she bent down to receive him in her arms. Rob and Sarah greeted Gloria then walked inside. It was eerie, but both of them felt like they had returned home.

Rob put down his briefcase in the alcove then gently pulled out a small wooden box. It was the gift Dr. Ryan had given him. He opened the cover. Inside were the set of Zeiss magnifying lenses, known for their durability, often outlasting the surgeons who wore them. Rob would likely use them countless times during his career, perhaps until the day he retired. An inscription was etched on the inside of the box cover:

From the Department of Surgery

Boston General Hospital:

Primum non nocere

Rob knew the Latin words, <u>primum non nocere</u>. They were attributed to Hippocrates, who practiced medicine over four hundred years before Christ. The phrase meant, *first do no harm.*

He couldn't wait to use his treasured gift while performing surgery at the Jamison Institute.

19

That evening after unpacking, Rob wanted to do something special. He proposed they splurge and go out to one of the nicer local restaurants for dinner. Although it was their first day back, Josh seemed so comfortable with Gloria that Sarah was willing to take Rob up on his offer. They changed, got into the Land Rover, and headed off. Minutes later they were at Señor Pepper's in the fancy downtown area known as Zona Dorada.

It was a gorgeous evening, and they were led to a table on the veranda. The sound of Flamenco music filtered through the air. The ambiance was sublime. They ordered a bottle of wine and sat holding hands. An onlooker might have thought they were newlyweds. As the waiter approached to take their dinner order, they heard loud voices and boisterous laughter. Rob tried to spot the location where the noise originated, but didn't have a clear view from where he sat.

Following a sumptuous main course, they shared a flambé of bananas Foster for dessert. As Rob paid the bill and prepared to leave, he once again heard loud voices. He looked in the direction of the commotion. Rob now had a direct view of the revelers. There was no doubt about it. Sitting at the rowdy table was the man in the red Porsche that had passed him at the Institute airfield, Dr. Ricky Pedraza. For a moment he was torn between leaving and walking over to say hello. Then, making his mind up, Rob took hold of Sarah's hand, and they headed toward Ricky's table.

The three couples sitting around the table were engaged in lively, animated discussion. Ricky had his arm around the shoulders of a beautiful woman at his side.

"Excuse me, Dr. Pedraza, I just wanted to say hello."

Ricky looked up at Rob. His expression left little doubt he was annoyed by the interruption.

"Yes?" Ricky responded.

"I'm Rob Sanders, and this is my wife Sarah. We ate dinner here and just wanted to stop by and say hello before we left."

Ricky thought for a moment before responding. "Ah, of course. How could I not realize? Dr. Jamison told me about you. You're from Boston General, correct?"

"Yes, that's right. We just arrived today. Tomorrow is my first day at the hospital."

"That's great," said Ricky responding with a smile. "You have no idea how much I've been looking forward to your arrival." Pedraza turned to the woman at his side and said, "A little more time off for me now that reinforcements have arrived." Ricky stood and held his glass aloft. He addressed the whole table, "May I propose a toast? To our new friends, Rob and Sarah, welcome to Mazatlan!"

Everyone took a drink, and there was a brief silence. Then the table once again erupted with rowdy talk and laughter. Rob saw several empty bottles of wine on the table.

"Would you like to join us?" Ricky asked. "I'll have the waiter bring two more chairs."

"No, thanks," Rob answered. "It's been a long day, and I need to be up early in the morning."

"Then, my friend, I'll see you at the Institute. We'll talk more then." Ricky stood to bid the Sanders goodnight. "It was a pleasure meeting both of you." Ricky bent down as he took Sarah's hand and gave it a gentle kiss then shook Rob's hand firmly. The newest citizens of Mazatlan left the table and walked out of the restaurant.

As Rob climbed into his vehicle, he wondered when Pedraza's first surgery was scheduled to begin in the morning. It was after midnight as they left, and it seemed the party going on at Ricky's table was going to continue for some time.

On the way back to the villa they opened the Land Rover's sunroof. In the short time since returning to Mazatlan, they had moved back into the beach villa they now owned, dined alfresco at an elegant restaurant, and were now driving home with a star-filled sky overhead. Life seemed about as good as it could get.

20

In the morning, Sarah drove Rob to the hospital. Pulling up in front of the hospital, she kissed Rob goodbye and wished him luck on the first day at the new job. Exiting the Land Rover, Rob took along the box with his Zeiss surgical lenses. Walking toward the entrance, he noticed a red Porsche parked in the doctors' lot. Rob thought, *That must be Ricky's.* The doors to the hospital opened, and he went inside.

Rob checked in at the security office where his photo was taken and an ID was generated. The card could be used to gain entrance to most of the areas in the hospital that were restricted. He had his thumbprint logged for biosensor entry to select areas in the research building.

Rob was introduced to the head of security, Octavio Vargus, who looked like a Mexican equivalent of Arnold Schwarzenegger. Vargus led Rob to the doctors' lounge and changing area. He gave Rob the combination to a locker assigned for him. Inside, he found a lab jacket with his name and the logo of the Jamison institute embossed on the front. "I'll leave you now, Dr. Sanders." Vargus told him, "I believe Dr. Jamison will see you shortly in the doctors' lounge. Any problems, just give me a page. Welcome to our medical staff."

Rob placed the box of surgical lenses into his locker then walked over to the shelves where the surgical scrubs were stored. He took a pair of the light-blue scrubs from the shelf and changed into his familiar uniform. The attire remained the same except for switching colors. The light blue of the Institute replaced the shade of green he had worn for the last three years at Boston General. When he thought about it, Rob realized he'd spent more of his time during the past few years dressed in scrubs than in street clothes.

Rob checked the surgical schedule posted on an LCD monitor in the lounge. He saw his name alongside Jamison's for the first case, a kidney transplant, on a patient named Victor Pina. It was set to begin in twenty minutes. Rob took a cup of coffee from the dispenser and sat down. As he began to sip from the cup, Jamison entered.

"Rob, I'm glad to see you." Before he had a chance to stand, Jamison held down his shoulder, preventing him from getting up.

"Relax for a minute and finish your coffee. I've got to go change into my scrubs. Then we'll go to the OR together. I'd like to introduce you to some of our staff."

A few minutes later, they walked to the operating rooms. They entered the one in which Victor Pina was being placed under general anesthesia. As he lost consciousness, the anesthesiologist inserted an endotracheal tube into his airway. Then the patient was connected to the ventilator so it could take over his respiration.

"Dr. Fernandez, meet our new transplant surgeon, Dr. Sanders."

Fernandez was focused on making some adjustments to the machine that was breathing for Mr. Pina. He looked up briefly and said, "Be with you in a second." After changing the settings on the machine's control panel, the anesthesiologist came forward to shake Rob's hand.

"Rafael Fernandez. It's my pleasure to meet you."

"Robert Sanders, but please call me Rob."

"Rumor has it you're from Boston."

Rob answered, "That's true. I did my transplant fellowship at Boston General."

"The only time I was ever in Boston was for an anesthesiology meeting at the Copley Plaza years ago. I had a good time for the few days I stayed in town. The seafood was terrific." Fernandez paused as he tried to remember something, "Legal Seafood, isn't that the name of the famous fish place? The Maine lobster is a hell of a lot bigger than the little ones we have down here. Anyway, glad to have you on board."

"The only problem with Fernandez," Jamison joked, "is that he falls asleep during cases, and his snoring can be distracting. I keep telling him to get tested for sleep apnea."

"Hey, enough of that," Raphael said, taking Jamison's humor in stride. "Let's get serious. Rob, do you have any preferences for music?" As he asked, the anesthesiologist opened a drawer that held dozens of CDs.

"Anything's fine by me," Rob answered.

"Good, then I'll make the selection for you." A few seconds later music by Fleetwood Mac started playing over the speakers.

In Rob's experience most anesthesiologists were as skilled in serving as operating room DJs as they were at rendering patients asleep for their surgery.

Dr. Jamison introduced Rob to the nurses in the room. Rob had already met the surgical technician, Don Adams.

"Rob, there's no medical school here in Mazatlan," Hal said, "and so there are no surgical residents or fellows to assist in the operating rooms. Down here we rely on our techs for help, and Don is one of the best. Hell, he could run circles around most board-certified surgeons. That's why I make sure to have him help me with difficult cases."

"Ah, Dr. Jamison, don't go embarrassing me." Adams said.

The kidney transplant on Mr. Pina progressed at a good pace as Jamison and Adams worked in tandem. It was clear to Rob that he was in the company of two experts. As the case continued they gradually relinquished most of the operating to him. When they were nearly through, Jamison broke scrub and walked out of the OR, leaving Rob and Don to finish up.

"It looked like you've been doing this sort of thing for a while," Rob said to Adams.

With his Texas drawl Adams answered, "Yes, sir. I've been working in operating rooms longer than I care to think about.

It'll be my pleasure to assist you on any case you want. Just give me a holler when you need me."

Jamison left the operating room to speak with the patient's family. Victor Pina was a third-generation Texan who owned an expanding chain of Mexican restaurants. He had enough money to have gone anywhere for his transplant but chose the Institute. When Jamison announced to his wife that the operation went well, she thanked him.

"Dr. Jamison," Victor's wife said. "In San Antonio it would take two years to get a new kidney with no guarantee, but here you found one for us in only two weeks! How can we possibly thank you?"

Jamison returned to the operating room area and found Rob. They walked down the corridor and stuck their heads into a room where two cardiothoracic surgeons were doing a heart transplant. Jamison said, "Guys, please say hello to Dr. Rob Sanders, our new surgeon."

They looked up from the opened chest of the patient lying on the table. In unison they answered, "Hi Rob," from behind their masks, then promptly returned to their work.

In the last operating room down the hall, Ricky Pedraza was finishing his case when Jamison and Sanders entered. Jamison spoke first.

"Ricky, I want you to meet Rob Sanders, our new associate."

Pedraza looked up from the operating table. Rather than engage in a lengthy conversation he responded curtly, "We already know each other. We met last night in the city." He looked back down and continued his surgery.

Then, as the two visitors were about to turn around and leave, Ricky asked, "Say, Rob, I hope you slept well last night. We've got a full schedule of cases awaiting you today."

"Don't worry," Rob answered. "I slept like a baby."

But Rob doubted Ricky could say the same. By the way Pedraza and his friends were celebrating when he and Sarah left Señor Pepper's, Ricky may not have slept at all.

As Hal and Rob walked down the corridor they ran into Sheila Morris.

"Welcome back, Dr. Sanders," Sheila said smiling. "I hope you'll be staying with us for a while this time around."

"I sure intend to," Rob replied.

Around noon Jamison told Rob to go to the cafeteria for some lunch. As he grabbed a sandwich and looked for a place to sit, he noticed Ricky eating alone.

"Can I join you?" Rob asked.

"Sure, but I won't be here long. I've been called off-site to operate on an organ donor."

"Are you rotating on the organ procurement team?"

"No, not really rotating. Adams and I are the procurement team."

"Ricky, if I'm not mistaken, I thought I saw you at the Institute airfield when I arrived on the flight in from Boston."

"I'm sure you're right. Don and I returned from harvesting some organs. In fact, I think the kidney I just transplanted was one of them."

"Don said you've been flying for some time?"

"Yes, since I was a kid. My father was in a business that required him to travel a lot by plane. He was an experienced pilot, so when I went with him, he'd let me take the controls."

Rob asked, "Where did you go to get the donor organs?"

"No need to worry about that now," Ricky answered, looking down at his watch. "Anyway, I've got to run. *Adios.*"

With that exchange, Ricky was up and out the door of the cafeteria. Rob's lunch meeting with Dr. Pedraza had come to an abrupt end. As Rob continued eating his sandwich alone, he thought, *Airplanes, sports cars; at least this guy is consistent. He likes things that move fast. But where is he going to harvest the organs?*

21

The first days working at the Institute went quickly. Rob was busy doing surgery and rounding on the postoperative patients. By the time his first week was over, he was ready for some time off. On Saturday, Sarah and Rob drove into Mazatlan with Josh. They explored the new city as a family. Walking through the town's central square, they sat on a bench, feeding pigeons that swarmed around them. At noon, they watched as young men at the waterfront put on a traditional show of bravery by diving off a precipice into the crashing surf below.

Returning home, they took a walk along the beach. Josh ran ahead of his parents, chasing the water's edge as it moved up and down across the sand.

On Sunday, Sarah and Rob decided to visit the recreational center, leaving Josh at home with Gloria. Sarah did her aerobics while Rob swam laps in the Olympic-sized pool. After Rob finished his laps, he laid in the sun on one of the lounges next to the pool. Nearly dozing off, he heard a voice from above.

"Hey, Doc, how are you?"

He looked up, but couldn't make out who it was against the glare of the sun. He propped himself up on one elbow and shielded his eyes from the sun with his hand. When his eyes adjusted, he realized that he knew the face.

"Oh, Don, it's you."

It was Don Adams, the surgical technician. "I didn't know you were a swimmer," he said.

"Well, I'm just getting back to it, but I used to be on the swim team in high school, about a million years ago."

Don laughed then added, "Best exercise you can do for the cardiovascular system, but I'm sure I don't have to tell you." Then Adams asked, "Well, how do you like our place in the sun so far?"

"No complaints. Everything has been outstanding." Rob asked a question of Adams. "So, Don, how'd you end up down here?"

"Oh, I used to be the chief technician at the animal lab at Baylor, same place as Dr. Pedraza trained. After he completed his transplant fellowship and set up shop here at the Institute, I got a phone call from him with an offer I couldn't rightfully refuse."

"Then you've known Dr. Pedraza for some time."

"Sure, we go back. He's a real character, isn't he? But he's got some of the best hands I've ever seen in the operating room. You know he comes from around these parts."

"No kidding," Rob replied.

"Ricky's dad is a wealthy man. He's big in real estate and owns some of the hotels by the beach. Ricky went to Guadalajara for medical school, but then did his surgery residency and transplant fellowship at Baylor. He got honors in everything all the way along."

"Don, let me ask you something. Since there isn't a national donor registry in Mexico, how do you get the organs you need to keep the program at the Institute going?"

"Oh, sure, procuring the donor organs. Ricky's in charge of arranging that." In the middle of his reply, Don told him, "You know, Doc, I'm running kind of late for an appointment. So I'll see you back at the hospital tomorrow."

Adams took off, leaving Rob poolside, still propped on his elbow. His rapid departure left Rob without a concrete answer to the question about the network the Institute used to procure its donor organs.

Rob was a huge proponent of organ donation. Back in the States, he not only signed on as a potential organ donor, but lobbied almost everybody he ran into about the values of organ donation. After all, the untimely death of a single person could save a score of others. One donor could give a heart, two lungs, two kidneys, a liver and a pancreas.

Rob couldn't understand why everyone wouldn't go along with the concept. The sad fact was that the vast majority of people never signed the agreement to serve as a donor. But there was little doubt that those same people would want an organ transplant for themselves or their family members should the need arise.

Sarah met Rob after she finished her workout, and they ate lunch together at the patio adjacent to the pool. When they returned home, Gloria left to spend the balance of the day at her home in the city. After Josh went to bed, they sat in their living room reading and relaxing.

Rob felt good about his job and family life. He had struck the balance he was looking for when he signed on with the Institute. For the first time in years, Rob felt content.

22

As the weeks passed, one of the things that impressed Rob most was the uncomplicated course of the postoperative patients at the Institute. None ever came down with rejection reactions or the serious infections he was so used to seeing back in Boston. The Institute's success rested with infusion of a solution containing the Chimera Factor protein that the transplant patients routinely received prior to surgery.

One evening Rob made his rounds later than usual following a long day of surgery. He stopped by to visit a patient scheduled for a liver transplant the next day. The room's lights were dimmed for the night. A bag containing Chimera Factor solution hung at the patient's bedside and was in the process of being administered. Rob noted it gave off an eerie bluish bioluminescence that seemed in character with its magical immune-altering properties.

As Rob finished his rounds and walked from the hospital, heading to the parking lot, a car nearly sideswiped him. Hitting the brakes, the driver backed up. Ricky Pedraza stuck his head out the Porsche's window and said, "Hey, Rob, sorry about that."

"No problem," Rob answered, although in truth he was pissed off at Pedraza's recklessness.

"See you tomorrow, *mi amigo.*" Ricky said, speeding off.

The next day Rob began his work day looking in on Bill Collier, an oil executive from Dallas, who came to the Institute for a pancreas transplant. Rob introduced himself to the patient he would be doing surgery on the next morning. Then, he explained the procedure in detail to his patient and offered to answer any questions.

"Boy," Collier said, "That's really something. I can understand you want to get the insulin from the transplant into my blood stream but hooking the pancreatic duct to my bladder that's pretty weird."

"Well," Rob explained, "insulin isn't the only thing the pancreas produces. The digestive enzymes it makes would eat up normal tissue if they didn't have a way to get out. That's why we hook the duct up to the bladder. So the enzymes will leave your body harmlessly in the urine."

The oil man laughed and said jokingly. "Jesus, doc, I'm spending $400 thousand bucks to end up pissing digestive enzymes in my urine. That's a hell of a deal."

"But think about it, you'll never have to look at the needle of another insulin syringe again."

"Yeah, I sure hope not. That's the reason I'm here. You go right ahead and hook everything up however you want, as long as I don't have to give myself another shot of insulin again."

Rob was shocked by the cost of surgery, more than three times what it ran at the General. It was the first time he'd heard a number quoted regarding a fee charged by the Institute.

Collier's preoperative infusion of Chimera Factor was almost completed when Rob said goodnight and left his room. Later, when the patients on the ward were asleep and all but a skeleton staff remained, Collier had another visitor. George Fleming walked into his room.

"Mr. Collier," Fleming said, "Sorry to disturb you. I just wanted to offer you the opportunity of participating in one of our current research studies. If you agree, you will receive a second dose of the Chimera protein before your surgery. Our experience indicates a significant benefit to your new organ. In fact, we haven't seen a single case of late rejection in anyone who has received the double dose."

"No kidding," Collier responded.

"Furthermore, if you participate, we'll refund a quarter of your costs and cut the check before you head back home."

"Say, that's not chump change when you're talking about what this costs." Then the patient asked, "Any bad side effects?"

"Not as far as we know." Fleming lied.

"Then show me where I sign on the dotted line."

Fleming handed him the permission form and pointed to the spot where Collier happily placed his signature.

The next morning, Rob proceeded with Collier's surgery. When he was ready to implant the pancreas, he asked the circulating nurse to show him the sheet of paper confirming the donor organ's blood type. Compatibility in blood types between donor and recipient was a basic requirement in transplantation. The nurse looked though the papers that accompanied the organ.

"Dr. Sanders, I can't seem to find the sheet with the blood type."

"Damn," Rob swore under his breath. "There has to be a blood type listing somewhere."

"I'm sorry, Dr. Sanders, but it's just not here."

Final verification was always the ultimate responsibility of the surgeon doing the transplant. Now without the document indicating the blood type, he was faced with a huge dilemma. Rob had his patient on the table with his internal iliac artery and vein exposed, awaiting connection to the new pancreas. The donor organ was floating in a bowl of chilled preservative solution directly in front of him. Rob swallowed hard, then did something he had never done before. He transplanted the pancreas without proper documentation of compatible blood type.

Fortunately, everything went well in the hours that followed the surgery. When Rob went to check on his patient in the SICU before leaving the hospital, Collier was already awake and breathing on his own. His laboratory measures and vital signs were stable. Rob left confident that Collier's surgery was a success. It wasn't until later that all hell broke loose.

Rob's phone rang at 1:30 a.m. "Yes?" Rob answered, half asleep.

"Dr. Sanders, Mr. Collier is having serious problems. You need to come right away."

The frantic tone of the nurse's voice told Rob he had to get to the hospital immediately.

"Sure. I'm heading in right now."

Rob stumbled in the darkness, trying to get dressed. He woke Sarah with the noise.

"What's going on?" she asked.

"It's an emergency with one of my post-op patients. I've got to go." He was at Collier's bedside in fifteen minutes.

The scene when he arrived was chaotic. Collier was no longer conscious. The breathing tube that had been withdrawn earlier had to be reinserted, and he was back on the ventilator. His skin had bruises everywhere that made him look like he had just been in a fight. Blood was oozing from around every intravenous site. The drain from his surgical wound was filled with bloody fluid.

"What happened?" Rob inquired as the adrenalin surged through his body. The nurse responded.

"Mr. Collier's monitor alarm went off, and we found he was having a lot of trouble breathing. We reinserted an endotracheal tube, then noticed he was bruised and bleeding all over."

Rob shot out a flurry of orders, "Send off a coagulation profile and a CBC with platelet count. Someone get me a flashlight so I can look in his eyes." He took the light and lifted Collier's eyelids so he could examine his pupils. His patient's eyes were looking blankly upward and his pupils were widely dilated. They didn't react to the bright light. "Shit," Rob muttered, "this can't be happening."

He knew what those dilated pupils meant. Collier had almost certainly experienced a massive intracerebral hemorrhage. If his brain swelling worsened, it could be fatal. Rob called out some additional orders.

"Start a mannitol drip, and give him ten milligrams of Decadron intravenously, now!" Rob prayed those measures would reduce the elevated pressure in Collier's brain. "Call radiology and get a stat CT scan of his head. Have two units of packed cells brought up from the blood bank and start transfusing them."

Transfusions were generally avoided after transplant because they might expose the patient to antigens in the blood that could later make chronic rejection more likely, but at this juncture Collier's life was in jeopardy. A transfusion was the least of his problems.

Within minutes, Rob's patient was taken down on a cart to the CT scanner. Rob watched as the images of Collier's brain came up on the viewing screen. A massive intracerebral hemorrhage had occurred in the left parietal lobe, and the surrounding brain tissue was distorted by all the swelling.

"Who's the neurosurgeon on staff?" Rob asked.

The nurse who accompanied his critically ill patient down to the MRI scanner responded, "We don't have a full time neurosurgeon here at the Institute. The last time we needed one we called in someone who works over at the city hospital."

"Do you remember the doctor's name?" Rob asked.

"I think it was Dr. Iberra. Yes, Hugo Iberra."

"Please try to get hold of him and see if he can come right away."

Within the hour Dr. Iberra was in the SICU. He carefully examined the patient and looked at the CT scan of the brain.

"His pupils are completely dilated, and he has no reflexes," Iberra said. Then he added with a somber tone. "I'm sorry to tell you this, Dr. Sanders, but there is nothing I can do to help your patient. He's already brain dead."

Rob felt the floor drop from under him. Only hours earlier, he was joking with the bodacious oil executive from Dallas, and now he was gone.

What the hell could have happened? Rob had witnessed death many times in the past, but couldn't recall a circumstance that caught him as much off guard as this. Iberra saw the anguished look on Rob's face and put his hand on his shoulder. Trying to console him, he said, "We all have a case go bad every now and then. Go home and get some rest. I'm sure you've got to be back at work like I do in a few hours. Feel free to call me at the city hospital when your mind is fresh, if you want to talk things over."

"Dr. Iberra, thank you for coming on such short notice. I really appreciate it."

The staff already started cleaning up the area. Soon Collier's body would be in the hospital morgue. From there it would be taken to a funeral home and prepared for its return to the United States.

Rob walked out of the hospital depressed. The adrenalin that had surged earlier had left him. He found it an effort to climb into the seat of his Land Rover.

When he arrived home, he quietly got undressed and climbed into bed. Sarah was sleeping soundly and had no idea of his return. Rob lay in the bed staring at the ceiling. Thoughts about Collier flooded his mind until he finally fell into a fitful sleep.

23

Rob arrived back at the hospital in the morning still upset and confused. No sooner had he entered the doors of the Institute than he received a page from Jamison.

"Rob, why don't you head on over to my office and have a cup of coffee with me?"

It was early, and Jamison's secretary hadn't arrived yet, so Rob knocked on the door to his office and let himself in.

"Good morning, Rob. Please have a seat." Hal gestured for him to sit in the chair facing his desk.

Steam was rising from a coffee mug waiting for him with milk and sweetener at the side.

"Go ahead and fix it the way you like it."

"Thanks," Rob said.

"I heard about last night and can understand that you're concerned about Collier's case. But, Rob, you're not new to this game. We all lose patients in our line of work. It's a reality we face every day as surgeons."

"I understand that, Dr. Jamison, but this is different. When I saw Collier before I left the hospital there wasn't any hint of a problem, plus from a technical standpoint the surgery went like a charm, not a hitch."

"Well, Rob, in dealing with complex biological systems, some-times things happen, which we just can't fully explain. That's probably the situation here. I know you were up most of the night and must be exhausted. Why don't you take the balance of the day off and get some rest. Come back tomorrow, and we'll hang some extra cases on your schedule to make up for today."

Rob wanted to say, *Forget it, I'm fine,* but in truth he was thoroughly drained. Rather than fight Jamison's suggestion he responded, "Sure, thanks." Then he got up slowly and left.

After he returned home, he trudged up the stairs to the bedroom, shut all the blinds and crawled into bed. Rob soon fell asleep for the balance of the morning. That afternoon, he swam and jogged along the beach. Later, still mulling over what happened with Collier, he decided to make a phone call. He called the hospital's SICU and asked for the nurse who had taken care of Collier the night before. When she came to the phone, he inquired, "I've been thinking about last night. Did you happen to notice anything unusual about Mr. Collier's vital signs before he deteriorated?"

There was silence on the end of the line. Then she answered, "No, everything was quite stable until after Dr. Fleming's visit around midnight."

"You say Dr. Fleming was in Collier's room late last night?"

"Why, yes, he went into Collier's room, and I saw him giving an additional dose of Chimera Factor. Because I'd never seen this done before, I asked him about it. He told me it was part of a new research project. As soon as the infusion was finished, Dr. Fleming was gone."

Rob wondered, *What was Fleming doing giving Collier an additional dose of Chimera Factor after surgery?* He had no clue, but intended to find out.

Rob picked up the phone and called the research building. He asked for Dr. Fleming, and the operator connected him with his office. The secretary informed him that Fleming had left town for several days. "Please have him call me as soon as possible," Rob requested.

Hearing the urgency in his voice, Fleming's secretary added, "If he should call in for messages, I'll be sure to have him contact you right away."

"Thanks," Rob said, putting the phone down.

There were too many unresolved questions floating around in his mind. Collier had bled from everywhere, but the fatal bleed was the one into his brain. It looked like a classic case of DIC, disseminated intravascular coagulation, where an inappropriate activation of the coagulation system took place. This depleted the factors that allow normal blood clotting to occur, paradoxically causing serious bleeding. But why should his patient suddenly develop DIC after a seemingly uncomplicated surgery? It looked suspicious that Fleming had given his patient an extra dose of the Chimera infusion without him knowing. Standard protocol was that a physician caring for the patient should be informed of the details to any research in which his patient was participating. Until he found out why that hadn't happened, he would not rest easy.

Early the next morning, Rob did something else. He picked up the phone and called the municipal hospital in Mazatlan. It was located on the opposite side of the bay from the Institute, about a twenty-minute ride without traffic.

"Could you please page Dr. Iberra for me?" he asked the hospital operator.

"*Si Señor*, please hold the line."

After a few minutes, a voice came on the line. "Hello, Iberra speaking."

"Dr. Iberra, this is Rob Sanders. I met you at the Institute hospital when you came to help out with my patient, Mr. Collier."

"Why yes, of course I remember. I only wish there had been something more I could have done for him."

"Well, you suggested that I call if I wanted to discuss the case further, and frankly there are still some things about his death that still bother me. Any chance we could get together and talk things over? Would you have any time later today?"

"Sure, I'll make some time, and the sooner the better. We should discuss the case while the details are still fresh in our minds. I should be done with surgery in the early afternoon. I have only two procedures scheduled for today. Tell you what, come to the city hospital after three o'clock, then page me from the information desk. And please, call me Hugo. I don't care too much for formality."

"That'd be great, Hugo. I'll see you then."

Rob left in the early afternoon and drove to the public hospital located in the southern part of the city. Along the way he passed the magnificent beaches of Mazatlan. Yet his thoughts were preoccupied with Collier's case, and he was anxious to speak with Dr. Iberra. Rob was heading to meet a man he didn't know well, but his gut told him he was a man of integrity, a man he could trust. Between Ricky's mysterious organ harvesting, Fleming's unexplained nocturnal visit to Collier's room, and the missing blood type documentation, Rob couldn't escape the nagging suspicion something wasn't right at the Institute. His conversation with Jamison did little to allay his concerns. He hoped Iberra would have an explanation that would put his doubts to rest.

24

Within moments of having him paged, Hugo Iberra appeared at Rob's side in the hospital's lobby. He warmly greeted his visitor.

"Dr. Sanders, welcome to our *Clinica del Publica*. It may not look as fancy a place as the Institute, but we know how to take care of sick people here all the same. Let's go to my office, so we can talk privately."

Iberra was a well regarded neurosurgeon and head of the surgical department. His office was on the first floor near the operating rooms. When they took their seats in his office, Iberra started in first. "You know, Rob, we could really use an MRI scanner like you have at the Institute. How fortunate it must be to have all the latest technology at your fingertips."

"That's one of the reasons I decided to take the job at the Institute. They have some of the best equipment I've seen anywhere." Rob went on. "I'm sure it wouldn't be a problem to send cases over to the Institute for an MRI. After all, your patients with head trauma that are declared brain dead surely have their organs harvested by the Institute."

"No, Rob, we have never been asked to supply any donor material. Actually, I've only been to the Institute once before in my life, and it wasn't so long ago. About two months ago I was called in for a case similar to Collier's. A woman with a recent kidney transplant suddenly started bruising and bleeding from her surgical incision. Then she developed right-sided weakness in her arm and leg. I took her to the operating room and evacuated a large blood clot that was compressing the left side of her brain. Although her neurological status improved, she just kept on bleeding from everywhere else and ended up dying."

Rob's blood ran cold on hearing about another case of unexplained hemorrhage at the Institute.

"You know, Dr. Iberra, I mean Hugo. I've been struggling with the thought of what happened the other night. Things just don't add up. Now that you mention a similar case, I have to wonder if there might be a connection."

"To be sure, there are a few things about the Institute that don't add up."

"What do you mean?"

"Well, when it first opened, people around here had great hopes that they might have access to the Institute's advanced medical services.

"Our working class people are not wealthy, and when the Institute first opened its doors they were kind enough to welcome them as patients for a nominal fee. But then funny things started happening. People who went there began to get complications, and some died after surgery without good explanation. All the while, the Institute was achieving great results for their wealthy clients who came from abroad. The locals began to think they were being used as human guinea pigs for research. Now, no one from around here uses the Institute. While I have no solid proof those allegations are correct, I have my doubts about the good intentions of the Institute."

Iberra continued, "Other strange things have happened. Some time ago a group of tourists came across a body in the desert not that far from here. We've had murders here before. God knows the local criminal gangs are a problem. No, the murder itself wasn't so unusual. It had more to do with the state of the corpse when it was found. It was missing all its internal organs."

"What?"

"Perhaps it's hard to believe, but the lungs, heart, liver, kidneys, and pancreas were gone. Very odd, wouldn't you say?"

"Sounds like a ritual killing or something along those lines."

"That was what the authorities suggested, but I've never heard of anything like that down here. I had my own suspicions."

"What suspicions?"

"I think the Institute had something to do with it."

"That's impossible," Rob said. "I can't imagine such a thing."

"Rob, I know the coroner, who performed the autopsy on the corpse. According to him the missing organs were removed with surgical precision, not just crudely hacked out as might be expected in a cult murder. A person with a medical background had to be responsible.

"I find that hard to believe."

"Rob, listen to me. Inside the chest and abdomen he found the arteries and veins were tied off with surgical ligature! This could only have been done by a person with considerable medical training."

"You cannot be serious about this."

"Indeed, I am. A toxicology screen on the tissues didn't find any cocaine or heroin. Instead, traces of a potent sedative, pancuronium, a paralyzing agent used during general surgical anesthesia, were discovered."

"So you think that somehow those bodies are connected with the Institute. But how would that make any sense?"

"Isn't the main job of the Institute to do organ transplant?"

"Are you suggesting someone was killed so that their organs could be taken for transplants at the Institute?"

"Rob, I can't say for sure. Perhaps he died or was killed for other reasons, but nonetheless the organs were taken. Although I have no proof they were used by the Institute, the circumstances are unsettling."

Rob was dumbfounded, but felt that Iberra would never make such a serious allegation capriciously.

"You must admit it's odd that Dr. Jamison never asked our hospital for help with providing potential organ donors when we sit less than ten miles from each other."

"I can't argue with you there, but then where do they get their organs?"

Hugo responded, "I don't know. All I can say is that I know of no legitimate network for organ donation. I've checked with colleagues at other hospitals around the region and they knew nothing about an organ procurement program."

Hugo paused for a moment and gave Rob a chance to digest the information he just heard. Then he continued, "Another strange thing. I saw a patient in the clinic who had a brain tumor. It was a slow growing benign tumor, a meningioma. His only symptom was a constant headache. While I was doing his preoperative examination, I noticed a scar on his flank. When I asked about it, he told me it was from an old stab wound. Routine blood work prior to surgery suggested a kidney abnormality. I did a CT scan and found only a single kidney was present. The one on the side with the "stab wound" had been removed.

The man told me that he had been jailed in the past but didn't tell me where. I couldn't get any more information out of him. He never showed up for his scheduled operation and disappeared without a trace. Now why would he leave town before I removed a tumor from his brain? I'm sure it wasn't because he was afraid of the operation. I think he was scared to tell me the truth about his missing kidney."

Iberra went on. "All these odd things were going on around Mazatlan. I hate to say it because you work there, but I think the Institute is involved."

Just then, Hugo's pager went off and startled Rob. Iberra looked down at the number on his pager. The call came from the hospital's SICU.

"Rob, I'm afraid I must leave to check up on one of my patients in the unit."

Rob got up to shake Dr. Iberra's hand. "Thanks for your time, and the information."

"Call me anytime you like. I always carry my pager." That was the last thing Iberra said as he took off for the SICU.

On his drive home, Rob couldn't help but come to the same conclusion as Dr. Iberra. There were too many odd things happening around Mazatlan. A dead body missing all its internal organs and a person whose kidney had been surgically removed but who was afraid to tell where it happened.

In the practice of medicine, Rob was trained to gather all the data then try to figure out a correct diagnosis. Now he was confronted with disturbing news coming from a credible individual that suggested the medical facility where he worked might be involved in unscrupulous activities. Could Jamison be buying the organs they used for transplant? Worse yet, were murdered victims unwilling donors? Rob needed to know the truth about what was going on, but he needed more data to reach the correct conclusion. Rob promised himself not to stop until he did.

25

Pat Hurley liked to be on top. After climaxing in a flurry of orgasmic shuddering, her naked body rested on Jamison's. She sighed with content and then rolled off. Sex with him had always been good. After their ten years together, nothing had deteriorated in the intensity of their lovemaking.

Pat remembered their first time. She had heard a rumor that Hal Jamison had an unhappy marriage. When they were introduced in Ryan's office, she sensed desire in his eyes.

Not long after that, she went to Hal's office in the research building to discuss next year's budget. It was after hours, and any staff had long gone. Pat sat across from Jamison and handed him a spreadsheet for his upcoming year's allocation. He scanned over the documents and had a question. Pat got up to come around on his side of the desk and examine the numbers Hal questioned. As she leaned over, her breast pressed against his shoulder, but she didn't pull back. Hal turned and looked up at her. He reached up and brought her mouth onto his. As they kissed, he got up from the chair. Each was pulling at the other's clothing, and in a minute they were undressed. Jamison led her toward the sofa he often napped on when working on his projects late into the night. When they finished, she and Hal lay there naked and sweating, breathing heavily from the frantic lovemaking. Hearing unexpected noise, the monkeys from the lab next door began howling in their cages as the naked lovers started laughing in response.

As husband and wife, they would have been divorced long ago. Individuals with personalities as strong as theirs would destroy each other in marriage. They kept the flame between them burning by their independence. Jamison was the most amazing man she had ever encountered. Nothing that transpired in the years since convinced her otherwise.

Pat Hurley was two years out from her MBA when she started working at the General. Her business skills were soon recognized. In a relatively short time, she was promoted to help manage the surgical department research foundation in collaboration with its newly appointed medical director, Dr. Tom Ryan.

Pat was considerably younger and undisputedly more attractive than Jamison's wife, Marlene, who was plain and not very ambitious. Hurley didn't view herself a seductress, just a better match for him. As Pat saw it, someone like Jamison deserved more. He was a brilliant surgeon and a visionary. Hal needed someone other than a mediocre partner. Sure, she had contributed to their breakup, but in reality it wasn't much of a marriage. It wasn't her fault Hal's ex-wife was such a loser.

It was a pity that they had not kept him on at the General. When things got sticky from the lawsuit, Ryan asked him to leave, rather than supporting his friend and his breakthrough research. Pat thought that deep down Ryan was jealous of her lover's abilities. For Hal it was an upsetting shock when his friend turned on him, but Pat decided to stand by her man. Together, they vowed not to let the setback keep them down.

Pat glanced at the time on the bedside clock. "Late, very late," she said. "I need to get to the office, but I'll make us some breakfast first."

As she got up from the bed, Hal called after her, "Some scrambled egg whites and a cup of strong coffee for me."

"Well, that's the least I can do for a man who just gave me a ride like that." Pat looked at Jamison, who turned over feigning to fall back asleep. She picked up a pillow and threw it at him.

"All right, I'll get up," he said, but Pat was already on her way out the door.

Hurley was the essence of efficiency. She knew Hal respected her consummate ability to get things done. Without her collaboration the Institute would never have become the success it was.

They were eating breakfast when the call came. Jamison picked up the phone. It was Vargus, head of security. "I had Jorge tail Sanders after he left the residential complex by himself yesterday. He went to *Clinica del Publica* where he met with Hugo Iberra. They were together for almost an hour before he left."

"I see," Jamison said with a concerned look on his face. "Thank you for the information, and please continue to keep a close eye on him."

"Yes sir, I will."

"What was that all about?" Pat inquired.

"Sanders was followed when he left for the city yesterday. Apparently he met with Dr. Iberra."

"Hal, I don't like it. Perhaps Sanders is too inquisitive for his own good. There's too much at stake to take any chances with him jeopardizing what we've achieved. We don't need another Wes O'Brien."

"Pat, relax. The boy has a healthy curiosity, and he's confused by some of the things happening around him he doesn't yet understand. The death of Collier really shook him. He's not one to lose a patient without a clear explanation."

"But there's no guarantee he'll be with us when he finds out the truth."

"Pat, don't worry. Didn't he choose to come here over rather than stay at Boston General or go to the Cleveland Clinic? Ryan's best and brightest rising star picked us. If only I could have seen the look on Tom's face when Rob told him he was going to join our staff.

I knew Rob would work with us the day I met him. When he watched me doing robotic surgery I could tell he was itching to use the device. Fleming told me he was like a kid in a candy shop when he visited the research facility. He couldn't believe his eyes when he saw the chimp with a human kidney. No, Pat, we don't have to worry. He's already one of us, even if he himself doesn't realize it yet."

"I certainly hope you're right."

"Of course I'm right," Jamison said, giving Pat a kiss on her cheek.

"I'll have Ricky develop a closer relationship with him. You know our Dr. Pedraza can be quite charming when he wants to."

Pat responded, "I'm not so sure that's such a good idea. They are such different personalities."

"To some extent that's true, but they have a common bond that's stronger than their differences."

"And what might that be?"

"Ambition!"

26

It was on a Saturday morning. Rob was off but he got up early and was swimming laps. As he did a flip at the end of the pool, Rob caught a glimpse of someone standing by the edge. Startled, he stopped his stroke and pulled off his goggles to see who the intruder was.

"Good morning," Ricky Pedraza said. "I thought I'd bring over a little breakfast for you and the family." Pedraza held out a bag he was carrying. "I heard the sound of you swimming from the driveway so I came back here first."

Rob hesitated briefly, then responded, "Heck, you just caught me by surprise, but sure, I'll go tell Sarah."

Ricky held his free hand out and helped pull Rob from the water. He hurriedly dried off and went into the house through the patio doors.

"We have a guest," Rob announced, calling up the stairwell to Sarah.

"Who is it?" Sarah returned from the upstairs bedroom.

"Ricky Pedraza, and he brought us breakfast."

"Oh, that's so nice of him. I'll be down in a minute."

Josh and Gloria were playing together in the family room. Rob walked up to them as Josh was putting the finishing touches to a tower made from Legos. He noticed Gloria's facial expression change when she saw Pedraza. Her smile disappeared. Gloria's body language told him that she not only knew Pedraza but disliked him.

A moment later, Sarah came down the stairs, hair still wet from the shower.

"Dr. Pedraza, what a pleasant surprise."

"I thought I'd bring my new associate and his family a special breakfast."

Sarah took the package from Ricky. "I'll make some coffee." Then she motioned over toward the table. "Dr. Pedraza, please sit down. Make yourself at home."

"Sure, but only if you promise to call me Ricky from now on. I never want to hear you call me Dr. Pedraza again."

"All right, I think I can manage that, Ricky."

"Terrific, then let's have some breakfast."

The three of them sat at the breakfast table and prepared to eat, while Gloria excused herself and Josh, since they had eaten earlier.

Ricky commented, "Better living here than Boston, don't you think?

Sarah responded first, "To tell the truth, I fell in love with this place on our first visit. The only drawback is that we're a bit far from family back in the States."

"That may be true, but that's what cell phones are for. Technology now even lets you see who you're talking with. That makes it easy to stay connected."

"You know, Ricky, you're absolutely right. In the short time since coming here, I've talked with my folks in Ohio more than I did during a whole year in Boston. At least it seems that way to me."

Ricky's friendly demeanor put his host and hostess at ease. Sarah thought, *He seems so nice, even if he initially came off as a bit of a playboy. How sweet to bring us breakfast.*

The small talk went on for the better part of an hour. Rob and Sarah learned that Ricky not only flew planes and loved driving sports cars, but that he had a speedboat as well. "And listen," Ricky told them, "any time you want, come on over to my place and take one of my cars for a spin, no problem. If you like, we can take the boat on a day trip to Cabo or Puerto Vallarta."

When Ricky departed, he left Sarah and Rob in good spirits. The surprise visit had shown him to be a much more affable person than either would have expected.

Rob walked out to the patio and joined Josh and Gloria who were outside. He sat on one of the chairs beside his housekeeper.

"Gloria, do you know Dr. Pedraza?"

"Well, Dr. Sanders, everyone in Mazatlan knows Ricky Pedraza."

"But, Gloria, the way you looked at him, I could swear there was more to it than that."

A moment of silence followed, after which Gloria said, "Dr. Ricky is an important person, and I don't want to say bad things about him."

"Gloria, think of yourself as one of our family. You should be able to tell me anything that's on your mind."

"This is difficult for me, Dr. Sanders, because I wouldn't want you to be upset with me for what I will say."

"Please, Gloria, go ahead. There's nothing more important than telling the truth."

She hesitated, but then spoke, "I've known about Ricky and his family for a long, long time. My mother worked for the Pedraza family when Ricky was a little boy, like Josh is now. Do you know Luis, Ricky's father?

"No, I've never met him."

"Well, in Mazatlan, Luis Pedraza is the *patron*. Although he now owns a lot of property, I've heard people say Pedraza is still involved with bad business, criminal things.

Luis began as a commercial pilot. Then he started bringing cocaine and heroin here from South America. Soon he began smuggling into the United States as well. My mother told me Luis took Ricky with him on his trips. That's how he learned to fly when he was very young." Rob listened intently as she went on. "Ricky's mother was a sweet woman who cried when Luis fooled around with other women and made no secret of it. He beat her when she complained. Eventually Luis drove her crazy."

Gloria began to sob and used her apron to dry the tear from her eyes. "Ricky's mother suffered until the day she took her own life."

"Jesus," Rob said. "That's horrible."

"My mother said that after she died, Señor Luis took over the soul of his son. Any goodness Ricky had from his mother was replaced by the evil of his father. *Luis es el Diablo;* Luis is the devil!" Gloria took a moment to regain her composure before she continued. "So now you can see why it is difficult for me to smile when I look at Dr. Ricky."

Rob was overwhelmed by Gloria's story. Never in a million years would he have placed Ricky Pedraza as the son of a Mexican drug lord. Ricky was a talented surgeon, a graduate of one of the best medical schools and surgical training programs in the United States. That Ricky learned to fly from his father while smuggling drugs strained reason, but there was nothing about Gloria that suggested she would tell lies.

Ricky Pedraza, who so thoughtfully brought them breakfast, the man who was his colleague at the Institute, had a father who made his fortune dealing in cocaine and heroin. Although he may have directed money to more legitimate enterprises like real estate, according to Gloria, Luis was still likely involved in trafficking.

Rob sincerely hoped Luis's son had nothing to do with his father's business, but in light of Gloria's revelation he had to wonder.

27

George Fleming was indeed a doctor, but not a doctor of medicine. He earned a PhD in biochemistry at Oxford with a specialty in proteomics, the study of proteins. While most attention was focused on genes, Fleming chose to focus on proteins. Once a specific protein was isolated and the sequence of amino-acids determined, it was relatively easy to work backward and construct the DNA sequence that gave rise to it. That was what bioengineering was all about. Then, using the DNA sequence and recombinant technology, you could synthesize the protein in large quantities.

Fleming thought the study of proteins would be the next 'big thing' in biological science, and he intended to capitalize on those discoveries. From Oxford, he traveled across the Atlantic to Massachusetts, where he ran a proteomics research lab at MIT. He spent his days using X-ray diffraction and computer modeling, analyzing protein structure or function, then trying to manufacture them in bioreactors.

Fleming and Jamison met purely by chance one evening following a lecture at the General given by Malcolm McCloud, a world renowned immunologist from the University of Glasgow. McCloud was giving a talk titled, "Cellular Chimerism and Immune Tolerance."

McCloud spoke with a thick brogue and began his lecture with a slide picturing a statue, the Chimera of Arezzo. He explained that the famous bronze was a piece of ancient Etruscan art unearthed in the town of Arezzo, Italy, in the year 1555. The strange creature it depicted had the head and body of a lion, but there was also the head of a goat arising from the middle of its back, and the lion's tail had the head of a snake at its end.

According to Greek mythology, the Chimera was a monster that spewed fire and wreaked havoc on the population. It was eventually slain by the warrior Bellerophon riding on his winged horse Pegasus. Some in the audience probably thought they had mistakenly wandered into a lecture on art history. Then McCloud further explained that the term chimera in medicine had come to mean a single organism that had genetically different tissue living within its body. He said, "Transplantation always creates a chimera since the tissue of the donor organ had different genes than the recipient."

McCloud went on to tell the audience about a series of exciting recent experiments indicating the transfusion of small numbers of white cells from an organ donor into the recipient had the ability to reduce rejection reactions and create a state of partial immune tolerance. "The answer to the problem of organ rejection," McCloud concluded, "is not in more potent drugs to suppress the immune system. Instead, we must achieve immune tolerance through a specific alteration in the defense system that Mother Nature gave us to fend off infections. If one of you here tonight can figure out the way to get the recipient of a transplant to recognize the foreign organ as self, you will not only have done a great service for mankind, but you will likely get a Nobel Prize in the process."

After the ovation, those with questions approached the professor. It was there that Hal Jamison and George Fleming bumped into each other. Afterward, they went for a drink at the Shamrock, an Irish pub located only a short walk from the hospital. Over pints of Guinness, a lively discussion ensued, which went on well into the night. Fleming was intrigued to hear about the immune tolerance capabilities of Jamison's stem-cell extract. At the same time, Jamison was impressed with Fleming's ability to isolate and sequence the amino acids in proteins.

Into their third pint, with lively Gaelic music playing in the background, Fleming and Jamison agreed to collaborate on their work. The new partners, a little unsteady on their feet, stood and held their glasses high. First, Jamison toasted, "To immune tolerance and limitless organ transplantation!"

Fleming's retort: "To proteomics!"

Their glasses clanked, sending the froth at the top flying.

According to their plan, Fleming would purify and analyze the protein in the stem-cell extract. By defining its amino-acid sequence and three-dimensional structure, he would learn a lot more about how the immune tolerance protein prevented rejection. In honor of McCloud's lecture, which had brought them both together, they decided to name Jamison's immune tolerance protein, "Chimera Factor."

When Fleming heard the news of Jamison's forced resignation, he was outraged, but there was nothing he could do other than offer moral support. Once Jamison and Pat Hurley firmed up plans to establish the Institute in Mazatlan, Hal asked Fleming to join his venture. Jamison offered him the directorship of the Institute's research facility and with it a salary larger than anything he could have dreamed of. George Fleming gladly accepted. He took an indefinite leave of absence from MIT and headed for Mexico.

Arriving in Mazatlan, Fleming set his sights on gaining independence from the stem-cell line for production of the Chimera Factor. He wanted to bioengineer the protein using recombinant DNA technology. This would be quicker and cheaper than purifying it from stem-cell cultures and also allow its unlimited production.

Once Fleming perfected a method for isolating the Chimera Factor protein, he began administering it to patients, and the organ transplant program at the Institute took off. Postoperatively there was no need for standard immunosuppressant treatment, and consequently there were none of the usual complications.

News of the Jamison Institute's remarkable success spread around the globe and wealthy clients flocked there to have their transplants.

Fleming found that Chimera could be used for organ recipients who had ABO blood-type incompatibility with the donor, a circumstance that normally would have precluded transplantation. However, it required a double dosing. In animals an additional dose of Chimera Factor caused no problems, but when he tried it in humans, bleeding complications occurred.

Perhaps a few patients had died during the experiments, but he reasoned that thousands would ultimately benefit from the results, so Fleming continued his work. Because the initial formulation he used could cause fatal hemorrhage, he made additional modification to the protein's sequence, one he was now convinced would avoid future problems. The substitution of a single amino-acid, a serine for an alanine, at position 163 along the protein's 180 amino-acid sequence, permitted it to work without a hitch. In fact, Fleming had already used the newly modified version of Chimera successfully in patients, including several who had unwittingly received their new kidney from a monkey instead of a human. None showed any sign of any rejection.

Using Chimera Factor, Fleming and Jamison had achieved a new paradigm in the ability to do organ transplantation. It would shake the foundations of medicine and make them very rich in the process.

George had just returned from Las Vegas. There he had met with representatives of interested pharmaceutical companies to update them on progress in his work with Chimera Factor. While he might have chosen any location in the world to hold his meeting, he chose Vegas. Fleming, like Jamison, had a passion, but it wasn't fly fishing or hunting. It was gambling. In Vegas he was able to play blackjack and craps while carrying on the business of the Institute. The circumstances couldn't have been more perfect.

Recognizing the significance of the Institute's work on immune tolerance, several pharmaceutical companies vied for the rights to the Chimera protein. Their money flowed into the Institute's coffers in the form of unrestricted research grants as they tried to cull favor. A portion of that money also found its way into Fleming's offshore bank account in Antigua.

George usually stayed at the Bellagio, occupying one of its luxurious penthouse suites. While in Vegas he was wined and dined by the suitor pharmaceutical companies in first-class style. On the day he arrived, a team of executives from Immuno-Logic took him to dine at Andre's in the Monte Carlo. They negotiated over a gourmet feast with wine flowing from bottles that cost hundreds of dollars apiece. After the meal Fleming bid the others goodnight and took a limo to Caesar's for some serious gambling at the blackjack tables.

It was after 1 a.m. when he arrived back at his hotel room. He showered, then relaxed, sitting on a sofa in the plush bathrobe provided by the hotel. He sipped on a glass of Courvoisier and looked out the suite's enormous picture window at the lights of the Vegas strip.

Fleming heard the doorbell to his suite. He got up from the sofa to answer it. There was no need to ask who was there. It was one-thirty in the morning, and he knew precisely who was waiting to enter. As Fleming opened the door, he heard Natalie say coyly, "Does this happen to be Dr. George's room?"

The gorgeous redhead was wearing a skintight skirt and a low-cut blouse revealing her ample cleavage. Natalie had the body of a goddess, perfected by plastic surgery. She stood a bit taller than Fleming in her high heels. Natalie wrapped her arms around his neck and kissed him before he had a chance to answer her question.

"Am I on time?" she asked.

"Of course you are, my dear. You always come on time," George quipped.

They both laughed as Natalie walked into the room carrying a stylish leather backpack from which she pulled a bottle of champagne. George went to his wallet and took out the money, which she stuffed into her backpack. Then, he sat back on the sofa and awaited his entertainment. Natalie was one of his favorites, and she always made him happy. That's why he continued to use her in spite of the $2,000-plus it cost for each encounter. She poured the sparkling liquid into each of two glasses until it bubbled over the brim. They made a toast then drank. Natalie went over to the stereo, put on a CD, and dimmed the room lights. As the music began, she walked to the picture window. The Eiffel Tower of the Paris Hotel stood majestically in front of her across the street.

"Are you ready?" she asked.

"As ready as I will every be." George answered.

Natalie hadn't quit her job as an exotic dancer for a lesser position. She had graduated from lap dancing at twenty bucks a pop to the big time. Natalie now made tons of money working for an exclusive clientele that included men, like Fleming, able to afford her special services. For the price she commanded, Natalie provided her patrons with the kind of experience they wouldn't soon forget.

Fleming spent most of his time in the lab, trying to bioengineer proteins to perfection. He didn't have the interest or personality for a meaningful relationship with a woman. Instead, he preferred liaisons with those on his list of high-class hookers. Following a day of intense business meetings, his routine was to relax afterward by gambling at the casinos then cap off the night with a prearranged party in the privacy of his hotel room. Luckily his income from the Institute and the money he skimmed from the pharmaceutical companies allowed him to pursue those interests.

With the music pulsating, Natalie began to undress in front of the picture window. Left clad in a G-string and garters, she continued to dance temptingly in front of Fleming, her silhouette illuminated in the mixture of moonlight and neon from the Vegas strip below.

Natalie moved closer to Fleming, who sat in quiet anticipation on the sofa. She began rubbing her body against him in ways that could never be attempted on her clients when she worked at the strip clubs. Then she undid the bathrobe he was wearing, and his body responded.

Natalie took a mouthful of champagne but didn't swallow. Instead she knelt down directly in front of Fleming, and her head went down between his legs. The action of her tongue and the Champagne's effervescence nearly brought him to climax. However, at just the right moment, Natalie stopped and got up from her knees. She climbed onto the sofa and straddled Fleming as he voraciously pulled her down onto him. The night was off to a good start. Before sunrise George had every intention of getting his money's worth from her.

By the time he staggered into his bathroom in the morning, Natalie was long gone. George had a luncheon meeting with Adelphi Pharmaceutical at the Venetian. He phoned room service and had some coffee sent up. He opened his briefcase and took out a stack of documents. He spread the papers out over the desk, organizing them in preparation for the meeting that would soon take place.

To this juncture, the drug companies knew that the Institute had a protein, which could induce tolerance to the major HLA antigens and therefore avoid rejection reactions without the need for potent immunosuppressant drugs. On this trip Fleming planned to disclose that the newly modified Chimera allowed successful transplantation even with ABO incompatibility, which would substantially expand the market for the protein's use. However, the real coup would be his news about animal organ transplantation, that Chimera Factor permitted human tolerance to animal organs and their alpha-gal antigen, which until now invariably induced fatal rejection reactions.

The Chimera Factor would have broad-reaching implications to the practice of medicine around the world. No longer would rejection be an issue for donor organ recipients, and transplant surgeons would no longer be limited to using human tissue. A surgeon would be able to transplant a baboon heart or a pig kidney. It would put an end to the long waiting lists.

The thought of all the organ transplants required in a world where the incidence of kidney failure, diabetes, and heart disease was skyrocketing made Fleming salivate. It would mean billions in revenue to the company that could provide the solution. George Fleming and Hal Jamison were in the position to sell the license for that solution as long as the price was right. With the final modification to the Chimera protein, the journey that began in Boston had been completed on the West Coast of Mexico at the Jamison Institute. The financial deal with one of the suitor companies would soon be consummated.

After Rob's first case in the OR, he received a call from Fleming's secretary informing him that he had returned to the Institute from his trip and would be available to meet with him. Rob was anxious to speak with him. He wanted to know more about what Fleming thought about Collier's death.

Rob entered the office as Fleming greeted him. "Rob, I'm so glad you stopped by. In fact, I've been meaning to talk to you about your research interests. Now that you've had a chance to get your bearings at the Institute, do you have any idea what you'd like to pursue as a project?"

"Maybe we could deal with that subject later. I stopped by for another reason." Rob went on. "Last week a patient of mine, Mr. Collier, had a pancreas transplant. The papers confirming the organ's blood type were somehow missing. After surgery, he started bleeding profusely from every incision and intravenous site. Then he bled in his brain. I had put in his new pancreas with no problem during the afternoon, and a few hours later he was dead. I thought you might be able to shed some light on the issue."

"Me?" Fleming questioned as he pointed at himself, his voice rising by an octave. "I didn't do the surgery. How could I be able to tell you about a complication?"

"One of the nurses from the SICU said she saw you in his room after surgery administering a second dose of Chimera Factor. It was after your visit that Collier started going downhill."

Fleming's face flushed. "Oh, that. That was the case where we needed to give a booster infusion of Chimera Factor."

"What do you mean?"

"Collier was part of a research protocol that called for a double dose."

"But for God's sake, why?" Rob exclaimed.

Fleming paused for a moment then went on. "Using an organ from a donor with unmatched ABO blood types requires an extra dose of Chimera Factor to ensure success."

"Unmatched ABO type, are you out of your mind? Nobody can transplant an ABO mismatch successfully. The rejection reaction to an ABO mismatch is overwhelming. It destroys the transplanted organ in hours and could kill the patient."

"Not here at the Jamison Institute," Fleming replied. "In our animal models, the double dose allows ABO incompatible grafts to take without rejection. Your patient Collier was on the list to have an ABO-mismatched graft as part of a clinical trial."

"You're telling me my patient was part of a research protocol that I didn't know about? Why wasn't I informed?"

Fleming glossed over Rob's question. "In point of fact, all the patients who come to the hospital are told before admission they may be called upon to participate in a research study. Patients are happy to help out because they realize the knowledge gained though our research allows us to offer them improved results." Fleming added, "I'm sure it's no different at Boston General."

"Results like Collier's?" Rob's anger was growing.

"All of our experiments with ABO incompatibility in animals indicated the extra dose of Chimera Factor is safe. Unfortunately, the double dose regimen in humans is sometimes associated with bleeding problems. I thought we had the problem solved, but Collier's case showed me an additional modification to the protein was necessary. That change has already been made. I can assure you there will be no more hemorrhages using Chimera Factor."

Rob asked, "May I see the consent form Collier signed?'

"Sure," Fleming answered.

He pulled a file from his desk, briefly shuffled through its papers, then handed Rob one of them. Rob scanned through the document.

"The risk of bleeding is not mentioned anywhere, and the offer of reducing the cost of surgery by 25 percent? This is hardly what I would call an appropriate informed consent; it's a combination of misinformation and financial coercion."

As he stood there talking to Fleming, the reality of what had transpired hit Rob like a ton of bricks. Not only had his patient been improperly dealt with regarding participation in research, but Rob himself had been unwittingly manipulated into doing the risky experiment on his patient. The waiver Collier signed would have never passed approval by any human studies committee. Fleming might be the head of a remarkable research lab and a brilliant scientist himself, but he was doing slipshod clinical work that violated the basic tenets of ethical human experimentation.

Rob was beside himself. He felt like jumping over the desk and wringing Fleming's neck. Accustomed to maintain a cool head during untoward surprises in the OR, Rob took a deep breath and glared at him with total disdain. Then, Rob stormed out of his office, slamming the door shut behind him.

The secretary sitting in the reception area was still in the middle of wishing him a good day when he walked past her without responding. Rob thought, *I've got to talk to Jamison as soon as possible. He's got to be informed of what Fleming is doing. This kind of research can't be allowed to go on.* Before Rob had even exited the building, Fleming was on the phone with Jamison. "Hal," Fleming said, "I think we have a problem."

28

Mazatlan had undergone a transformation since Jamison first visited there a decade before with his former wife, Marlene. It had grown into a bustling metropolis whose population swelled to over one million during tourist season. Although he would have much preferred a vacation in Wyoming to go fly-fishing, in deference to his wife's relentless nagging, he agreed to a trip she arranged in Mexico. Marlene hated his fishing expeditions, perhaps rightfully so, since each day he would be off with his guide before dawn, and she wouldn't see him again until evening. She was resigned to spend most of the day alone, reading books while fighting off mosquitoes.

In Mazatlan, Marlene soon realized it was impossible for Hal to simply lie on the beach and relax. In an effort to appease him, she suggested they go deep-sea fishing. At least that way she could spend her time sunning on the boat. Unfortunately, Hal became terribly seasick, and they had to return to shore prematurely. Afterward, he vowed never to try deep-sea fishing again.

They stayed at the hotel Ocean Breeze on Avenue Del Mar near the quaint old section of the city. One evening while they were having dinner at the hotel restaurant, one of the patrons became ill. While eating lobster she developed difficulty breathing. At the same time her tongue and lips swelled grotesquely, distorting her face. Within minutes of her symptoms starting, she turned blue and helplessly clutched at her throat trying to breathe.

Hal heard the commotion coming from a nearby table and was at the stricken woman's side in a flash. He recognized that she had most likely suffered a severe allergic reaction to the shellfish, causing the larynx to swell, cutting off her air supply. She was losing consciousness, and he had to act fast. While the others looked helplessly at the woman suffocating in front of their eyes, Hal knelt next to her and produced a small Swiss Army pocket knife he had on his keychain. An emergency tracheotomy was the only option.

Hal pulled open the blade. He positioned its tip just below the woman's Adam's apple, identifying the level of the cricothyroid membrane by touch. Then he jabbed the blade tip into her neck. It penetrated less than an inch to enter the trachea. He turned the blade sideways to create a small opening, but the unconscious lady was no longer making any effort to breathe. He had to get air into her if she was to survive.

Hal saw the waiter standing near him and shouted, "Give me your pen!" With a trembling hand the startled waiter pulled the ballpoint from his shirt. Hal quickly separated the top and bottom of the pen, removing the inner cartridge. Then he worked the hollow tip into the hole in her neck, creating a makeshift endotracheal tube. He took in a deep breath and blew hard into the exposed part of the pen, inflating her lungs. He repeated the forced inflation again. The woman coughed and began to move. She started to breathe on her own through the new airway. Her blue face soon began to turn pink again. She opened her eyes. Hal saw the look of confusion and fear.

"Just take it easy," he told her. "You've had a bad allergic reaction to the shellfish you ate, but you'll be fine. Don't try to speak. There's a tube in your trachea helping you breathe."

His reassuring words and firm touch reduced her panic. She continued to breathe on her own as Hal held the tube in place. An ambulance arrived a few minutes later. There was no doubt in anyone's mind that the woman would have died had Hal not intervened. The paramedics placed an intravenous line in her arm and administered a dose of Benadryl, epinephrine, and the steroid Solucortef. In response to the drugs, the facial and lip swelling began to abate by the time the paramedics prepared to leave for the hospital. Hal walked next to the cart holding his patient's hand as they carried her to the ambulance waiting at the front of the hotel. The woman's husband came over to Hal and thanked him profusely.

"I can't believe this happened," he said. "We eat fish all the time. She never had any problem before."

"Well, just make sure she never has lobster or any another shellfish in the future. I'm staying at the hotel, so please give me a call and let me know how things go at the hospital. Hopefully she won't have to be in the hospital for more than a day or two. By the way, I'm Dr. Hal Jamison."

"Thanks again, Doc."

With that, her husband boarded the ambulance for the ride with his wife over to the city hospital.

Hal washed the blood off his hands then returned to Marlene at their table. Not long afterward a distinguished looking man walked over and thanked Hal for his help. He insisted on taking the check for their meal. The man introduced himself. "I'm Luis Pedraza, owner of the hotel. I want to thank you for helping that poor lady." Luis motioned to the waiter. "Pablo, bring a bottle of our best champagne for these guests."

A minute later the waiter returned with the chilled bottle, which Luis himself opened and poured for Hal and his wife. Hal graciously invited him to join them at the table for a drink, and Luis sat down. When he learned that Jamison was a transplant surgeon at Boston General, Luis declared, "Ahhh, Boston General. I hear your hospital is one of the best in the world."

"You're too kind, Mr. Pedraza," was Jamison's reply.

"My son, Ricky, is finishing medical school in Guadalajara. How ironic, his ambition is to become a surgeon. To imagine that someday he could save someone like you did."

"Oh, I'm sure he'll be able to do that and much more," Jamison responded. From the time of their fortuitous encounter, the two men began a relationship that ended up outlasting Jamison's marriage.

At Luis's invitation Hal returned to Mazatlan on a number of other occasions. After his divorce from Marlene, he brought Pat along, who worshiped the sun and loved the beaches of Mazatlan. They usually stayed as personal guests of Pedraza at his luxurious estate.

When the time came for Luis's son to apply for a residency, Jamison made a phone call to the chief of surgery at Baylor on his behalf. Although Ricky Pedraza was a good student, it was Hal Jamison's recommendation that got him accepted into the highly sought after program.

Following the abrupt departure from Boston General, Jamison and Pat Hurley traveled back to Mazatlan, only this time the trip was not for pleasure. Hal had developed the concept, and Pat the financial projections, for building a transplant center in Mazatlan. They met with Luis, and she made her case for constructing a world-class medical facility for organ transplantation, which would service only those persons wealthy enough to afford its steep price.

She told Pedraza, "Why should someone have to go to an obscure town in Pakistan or China to buy an organ, then have some mediocre surgeon put it in? People will flock to an institution on the Gold Coast of Mexico run by a famous American surgeon from Boston, and they'll pay top dollar. Once word spreads that our results are superior to those of the finest hospitals in the United States and Europe, there'll be a waiting list of wealthy international clients a mile long. We'll make a fortune!"

Hurley told Pedraza how the stem-cell extract that Jamison discovered could prevent organ rejection and its enormous potential value. She told Pedraza, "Given proper funding, Hal can bring in a team to continue working on the immune tolerance protein. Eventually, the rights for its commercial production could be sold to a pharmaceutical company. A product like that could be worth a hundred million or more!"

Pedraza listened to Hurley making her pitch. When she was finished, he remained silent. Then, he pulled out a Cuban cigar from his shirt pocket, clipped the end off, and lit it. He took several deep drags to get it going. As the thick smoke he exhaled cleared from around his face, Pat saw a broad smile. Luis spoke while nodding in approval, "You know something, Patricia, I like that idea. I like it a lot." And thus, the Jamison Institute was born.

Pedraza was a ruthless gangster, but also a businessman who had vision. He began his career as a commercial pilot flying cargo across Latin America. Later he supplemented his income by transporting a little contraband, like drugs or guns. Before long he started his own small operation and quickly rose to the top, burying a host of competitors along the way. Now he was known by cartels throughout South and Central America as the man to talk with if you needed product transported to the United Sates. In fact, business in shipping drugs had substantially improved since the Institute came into being. His jet with the prominent emblem of the Jamison Institute on its fuselage provided the perfect cover. Who would think that in some of the boxes of medical supplies were hidden kilos of cocaine?

Some time back, Pedraza decided to diversify his assets and venture into real estate. He purchased what was regarded as the best hotel in the city, the Ocean Breeze, and bought several apartment buildings along the waterfront.

Years back, when Jamison and Hurley first came to him and pitched the idea of his funding a transplant Institute in Mazatlan, Pedraza carefully considered their offer. He thought it might be wise to extend his financial operations into the recession-proof area of medical services. He reasoned there would always be people who got sick and needed help regardless of the prevailing economy. Moreover, if his drug business slowed because the authorities put pressure on his trafficking, he could fall back on the medical business. The more he thought about the concept of the Institute, the more he liked it, so Luis committed the funds for the construction of an exclusive transplant center in Mazatlan.

During their meeting he shook hands with Hal and Patricia and called for a servant to bring them a bottle of champagne. He raised his glass to make a toast. "To the Jamison Institute, the best transplant hospital in the world, right here, in Mazatlan!"

When Hal Jamison took Fleming's call and heard his anxious tone describing the meeting with Sanders, he told his old friend, "You're overreacting to the situation. Rob is destined to be the most loyal and energetic associate we have at the Institute. Just give him a little more time and stop worrying so much." Hal went on. "Let's face it, George, you're mainly in this for the money, but Sanders wants more than that. He wants to save humanity. In the larger equation, he'll conclude that the loss of a few lives to save so many others will be more than justified."

Fleming seemed to calm with Jamison's reassurance, "Hal, I hope you're right," he said, before putting down the receiver.

29

Jamison entered the private lab he called his 'pet shop.' He was welcomed by the sound of the animals stirring in their pens and cages. Usually he went there to perform surgery, but sometimes just to visit. Seeing the creatures that were born of his imagination lifted his spirits. The patients he operated on at the hospital always left after their brief recovery. They flew back to Hong Kong, Paris, Buenos Aires, or wherever with their new organ, never to be seen again. However, the animals in his lab, testaments to his brilliance at transplant surgery, and the immune tolerance protein he discovered were always there.

Visiting reinforced Jamison's sense of purpose and allayed any sense of guilt. If he ever had second thoughts concerning the sacrifice of persons who died in the course of developing the Chimera Factor, he had only to swing by the lab and see his 'pets.' The animals were combinations of different species surgically melded into one body and, thanks to treatment with Chimera Factor, none showed any signs of rejecting their newly implanted body parts.

When Jamison came to visit, he would often bring special treats and feed them. The goat-dogs were among his favorites. The stroke of surgical genius that allowed him to make this chimera was credited to Adams. Using Jamison's organ preservative solution and miniature pumps, Adams devised a method to keep the head of an animal alive, separated from its body, for a period of time. It was long enough to connect the head's arteries and veins onto vessels emanating from the back of a host animal.

Then he anchored the transplanted head's neck muscles to the host's vertebrae. There was no need for lungs or a digestive system since the nutrients and oxygen for the head were all supplied by the arteries of the host animal which did the breathing. The cranial nerves were left intact and could function normally, so the transplanted heads could see, hear, and smell. They could move their eyes, tongues, mouths, and even turn their heads to some extent. However, because they lacked air moving through their vocal cords, the transplanted heads were silent.

Jamison's favorite was a different kind of chimera. Tom was a chimpanzee he named after his previous friend and colleague in Boston. Jamison gave him human arms that were attached with the assistance of Adams in a complex surgical procedure that had lasted nearly twenty-two hours.

After the operation Jamison took great pains to assure the chimp's recuperation. He slept in the lab for the first three nights to make sure nothing went wrong. Later, Hal often stopped by to feed and groom him, since his patient couldn't use his own arms for weeks following the surgery. Hal would take Tom out of his cage and cradle him in his arms, as if he were his own child. When all the bandages were finally removed, Jamison couldn't help but notice the quizzical expression on the primate's face at the sight of his new limbs.

When Tom's rehabilitation was complete, Jamison had achieved more than he might have rightfully expected. The chimp had full use of his new arms, and his hands could maneuver with near human dexterity.

Unfortunately, over time, Tom didn't take well to having the weaker hairless arms of a human in spite of what he could do with his hands. His resentment grew to such a degree that he had to be kept in his cage lest he attack Jamison. During his visits Jamison was resigned to sit in a chair in front of the chimp's cage and talk to him at a distance.

"Don't you realize I saved your life?" Jamison asked Tom. "Fleming would've given you a human kidney, then a few months later chopped you up so he could look at the pieces under a microscope. Why be upset with me?" Jamison appealed for Tom's understanding. "I gave you human arms and hands so you can do things no ape in the history of the world has ever been able to do." Jamison paused for a moment then asked, "What do you think about that?"

In response, Tom, who had been sitting quietly, while munching on some fruit, suddenly gave out a shriek and jumped onto the bars of his cage. He snarled at Jamison, exposing his sharp incisors. If the bars hadn't held him back, Tom would have sunk them into his visitor's neck.

"All right, be that way," Jamison said. "But I certainly hope your attitude improves soon. Otherwise, I'll be forced to feed you a diet of tranquilizers to keep that nasty temper under control."

Jamison got up from his chair and walked past the cage. As he did, the ape reached his human arm out between the bars, attempting to grab him. Luckily for Jamison, he was just beyond Tom's reach.

In spite of the primate's hostility, Hal felt invigorated by his visit. No one had ever been able to achieve what he had done. It was only a matter of time until the world would give him the recognition he deserved.

Jamison left the research building and headed back to the hospital that bore his name. There was a liver transplant being prepped for the OR, and he was scheduled to do the surgery within the hour.

30

Rob called Jamison's office to request a meeting. His secretary responded, "Why, I'm sorry, Dr. Sanders, but he's gone out of town. He flew to Wyoming early this morning. But I'm glad you called, because I was just about to page you. Before he left, Dr. Jamison insisted you join him for the weekend in Jackson Hole. Jorge will pick you up at eight o'clock tomorrow morning and take you to the airfield. The Institute jet departs at nine."

When Rob returned home that evening, Sarah could see a look of distress on his face.

"What's wrong, Rob? You look like something terrible happened."

"Something is very wrong, but I'm still trying to put all the pieces together. Remember the patient who died last week after his pancreas transplant? He was given an extra dose of Chimera Factor by Dr. Fleming as part of an experiment I knew nothing about. Moreover, the organ I transplanted into him wasn't labeled and turned out to be an ABO mismatch. Fleming manipulated me into doing a surgery I never would have performed had I known all the facts."

"Rob, are you sure? That's a serious charge."

"Yeah, it's pretty damn serious when you place someone's life at risk just to get data for a research project you haven't properly informed the patient or his physician about."

"There must be some explanation. You should take the issue up directly with Dr. Jamison."

"That's just what I intended to do when I found out he left for his place in Wyoming. His secretary requested I join him there for the weekend. The Institute jet will fly me to Jackson Hole first thing tomorrow."

"Rob, that sounds like a good idea. You'll have time to hash things over without the distractions of work. Let's go upstairs and get you packed. By the way, don't forget to take your fishing rod."

"What fishing rod?" Rob asked in earnest before he got the joke. Seeing her smile, he laughed and felt his tension ease. He'd go to Wyoming for the weekend for some fly-fishing and a frank talk with Jamison, if that's what it took to resolve the concerns he had about Fleming's brand of human experimentation.

The jet carrying Rob landed at the airfield just outside of Jackson Hole. His ride was waiting for him when he arrived. Ernie, the driver, put Rob's bag into the back of the SUV. He told Rob it would take about thirty minutes to reach Jamison's ranch. Ernie headed down Highway 22, coursing parallel to the mountain range.

"Man, this place is incredible!" Rob exclaimed, looking out the window at the majestic snowcapped peaks.

"I take it you've never been here before?" Ernie was used to hearing that from visitors who saw the Grand Tetons for the first time.

"No, I've never been to Wyoming."

Ernie continued. "Well the Tetons are special. There's nothing like them anywhere else in the world. They rise clear up to the sky right out of the ground, no foothills. In fact, the French explorers who first saw them gave them their name. 'Teton' means 'breast' in French."

A few miles up the highway, Ernie turned onto a private road that led to Jamison's home. The ranch and its lodge sat along the bank of the Snake River with the mountains in the background.

Ernie managed Jamison's property, which he told Rob consisted of four hundred acres. As they approached the lodge, Rob could see it was a massive structure.

"Wow," Rob exclaimed.

Ernie responded, "Another home about a mile from here sold for ten million last year. It was only half this size and on less land. This one's got to be worth at least double that." As they entered, Ernie directed Rob into Jamison's study, which stood just off the great room. The study resembled Jamison's inner sanctum at Mazatlan, only larger. Many species of local game were represented on its walls. The heads of a moose, elk, mountain goat, and black bear silently glared down at him. A gun cabinet stood against one wall and there was also one containing crossbows, Jamison's preferred weapon for hunting. A worktable used for making fishing lures was against the far wall.

Jamison's desk was a massive piece of mahogany in the center of the room. Rob noticed that on it stood the same strange bronze sculpture he had seen in Mazatlan, a facsimile of the mythological Chimera.

Jamison wasn't there when he entered, so Rob made himself comfortable on the sofa. His host walked in a few minutes later.

"Rob, you're here already. Terrific, glad you came." Hal went over and warmly shook his guest's hand. "Can I offer you something to eat?"

"No, I'm good. I had some food on the plane, so I'm not really hungry."

"Well, let's get you something to drink. Remember, we're up a few thousand feet in elevation, and it's best to keep well hydrated." Jamison pressed the intercom and placed a call to the kitchen. Some bottled water and a bowl of fruit arrived a few minutes later.

"Have a chance to take in the view while you were waiting?" Jamison asked, pointing at the enormous picture window that the sofa faced.

"It's extraordinary," Rob said.

Jamison noticed a man appear out of the shadows at the entry to his study. "Luis, come over here. Let me introduce you to my new associate, Dr. Sanders."

The man stepped forward and shook hands with Rob, "Hal has nothing but good things to say about you. I'm Luis Pedraza. I think you must know my son, Ricky."

"Yes, of course, we work together. But how do you and Hal know each other?"

Luis looked at Hal then Jamison answered for his friend. "That happens to be a long story and would probably bore you."

Meanwhile, Luis made his way over to Jamison's desk and opened a humidor, pulling out a cigar.

"Anyone care for one?" he inquired, looking at Hal and Rob who declined his offer.

As Luis lit his cigar, Rob recalled Gloria's story about Pedraza's wife and his involvement in drug trafficking.

Jamison said, "Rob, why don't you unpack and get settled in? Let's plan on driving into town for dinner around seven."

For dinner the three had a meal of bison steak, accompanied by several bottles of good wine at one of Jackson Hole's best eating spots. The restaurant's owner appeared to know Jamison fairly well—well enough to ask how Pat was doing and to address him as "Doc."

By the time they made it back to the lodge, everyone was tired and decided to hit the sack. Before he fell asleep Rob promised himself that the issue of George Fleming's human research would definitely be on the agenda for discussion tomorrow.

31

Ernie and Luis took shotguns from the gun cabinet and left before dawn to go hunting. Jamison was in the kitchen when Rob entered, and they had breakfast. After their meal, both prepared to go fishing.

They packed up gear, threw it into the back of an SUV, and Jamison drove them down a trail along the river. When he arrived at the selected spot, they stopped, donned thigh-high wading boots, took fly-fishing poles, and walked into the water.

Jamison's vest was covered with an impressive array of fishing paraphernalia. He had an assortment of flies and tools hanging from every part. There was even a surgical hemostat clipped on for emergency use in the event a fly needed repair. Standing in the strong current of the Snake, Jamison was as much in his element as in an operating room. The graceful motion of his casting was a pleasure to watch. Rob, a novice, was having some difficulty so Jamison went over and demonstrated how he needed to flick his wrist and release the line simultaneously. In no time, Sanders was casting like a pro, and found himself falling under the spell of nature's beauty. As the cold water swirled around his boots and the sun glistened off the river's surface, Rob felt an intoxication he had never experienced before. He began to understand Jamison's passion.

The serenity was broken when Rob's line became snagged in a tree branch that hung low over the water. Jamison trod to the rescue and freed the entangled line. After using his hemostat to repair the bent fly, Rob was back in business. They worked their way upriver to one of Jamison's favorite locations. It stood just below a short run of rapids.

"Rob, cast over there where the water slows. That's where the big ones like to spend most of their time."

Taking Hal's advice, Rob threw his line and soon had his first strike. Rob worked hard at reeling in the fish that continued to fight until Jamison scooped the large cutthroat trout into his net.

"Way to go, Rob!" Jamison exclaimed. He took pliers from a pocket on his vest and removed the hook from the trout's gaping mouth. Jamison handed the fish to Rob who held his prize while admiring its shimmering coloration. Then, Jamison took it back and gently let the fish slide into the water. They watched as it swam to freedom.

The hours passed quickly. When Jamison decided it was time to leave, Rob would gladly have stayed longer. Rob followed Hal ashore, where they took off their boots, undid their rods, got into the SUV, and drove back to the lodge.

Rob returned with a good appetite, the product of fresh mountain air and exercise. The feeling of fatigue surprised him. Walking in the river current while trying to maintain balance on the slippery rocks took more energy than he expected. They ate lunch and, after finishing the meal, Rob brought up the subject of Fleming's experiment.

Rob began, "Hal, there's something I've been meaning to talk to you about."

"Sure, Rob, shoot."

"Well, it's about Mr. Collier, the patient who died after his pancreas transplant. One of the night-shift nurses told me she saw Fleming go into the patient's room after surgery and give him an extra dose of Chimera Factor. Not long after that he started bleeding everywhere, including into his brain."

"What an unfortunate complication," Jamison remarked.

"Well, I believe it was the extra dose of Chimera that somehow triggered the bleeding. I also think that Fleming removed blood type information from the donor pancreas so I would do the surgery without knowing I was transplanting an ABO-incompatible organ. In addition, the consent form Fleming showed me that Collier signed was a misrepresentation."

Rob went on. "Fleming chose to ignore basic principles of ethical human research, and my patient died in the process. I can't let that go unanswered."

"Rob, I'm sure you realize that the many achievements you saw at the Institute are the result of an extraordinary research effort. Because of our devotion to medical progress, projects at the Institute move along faster than they ever could back in the States. As I see it, the less time between basic research and its clinical application, the more lives will be saved in the long run. The sooner we can get our work out of the laboratory and to our patients, the better. At any rate, no laws in Mexico regulate research projects like back in the States. In spite of that, we've created our own institutional review board to oversee human experiments and make sure the projects are compatible with international standards. That review board signed off on Fleming's project. It was just an unfortunate oversight that you weren't informed."

"Can I ask who sits on the board?"

"Sure. It consists of me, Pat Hurley, and Dr. Fleming."

Rob thought, *What? George Fleming on a review board? That's a fox guarding the chicken coop.*"

"Rob, your patient Collier signed a document giving his permission to participate in our research protocols. Unfortunately, he had an unforeseen complication. I can see you're upset, and Fleming should have discussed it with you ahead of time. I'm sure we can make adjustments that will prevent anything like this happening in the future."

Rob seemed to settle down after Jamison's statement. Hal went on. "Let me take this opportunity to share some important information with you. Our work with the immune tolerance protein has entered a critical final phase. Fleming's latest achievement has given us a solution for overcoming the problem of ABO incompatibility. The newly modified protein doesn't produce excess bleeding even at higher dosage. Fewer persons will have to wait as long for a donor organ if ABO compatibility no longer matters, and consequently more lives will be saved."

Jamison told him, "Rob, as you know, the alpha-galactose antigen is the chief reason humans reject the organs of other mammals."

He continued, "Obviously the ability to successfully transplant animal tissue would be nothing short of a godsend. Thousands upon thousands of people would be spared death and disability because they couldn't get a transplant in time. All the registry lists around the world could be torn up and thrown away. The extra dose of the modified Chimera is all that will be required to overcome the problems with animal donors."

Jamison sensed that the tide turning in Rob's mind. He was doing a good job selling his program, and his junior associate was buying into it.

"Rob, let me tell you something else about George Fleming. Whatever your impression, the man is a brilliant researcher and always has the best interests of humankind at heart. He worked day and night to modify the Chimera protein so bleeding complications will no longer haunt us. Here, come over to the computer and let me show you something interesting."

Rob walked over and faced the computer screen. Jamison called up an image of the three-dimensional structure of the Chimera protein on the screen. It had the appearance of a large, twisted pretzel. With another click on the mouse Jamison created two colored regions along the length of the protein, one purple and one green.

Jamison explained, "The Chimera Factor has a sequence of 180 amino-acids and also contains two disulfide bonds that fuse different parts of the protein together, creating the complex three-dimensional structure you see on the screen. The green overlay shows the 'active site' that consists of only ten amino acids. This is the area that binds to a receptor on white cells and mediates the immune tolerance effect."

Hal Jamison pointed to another portion of the protein on the computer. "This purple region, consisting of six amino acids, causes the bleeding problems by activating the coagulation system. Fleming has successfully modified the protein by changing only one of the amino acids at this site. In point of fact, no one since Collier has had a hemorrhagic complication. Rob, you have my word, there will never be another case of serious hemorrhage."

As Rob was thinking, Jamison continued his effort to bring him over. "You, better than anyone, should realize what all this means. The benefits of transplantation will see broader application, and humanity will be saved from much unnecessary disability and death. Look, once we get back to the Institute, I'll ask Fleming to begin drafting a protocol for animal organ use in humans and make sure he gets your approval before any cases are attempted."

As Jamison was concluding his argument supporting Fleming's work, Luis and Ernie returned. Luis walked into the study carrying his rifle on his shoulder, while smoking a celebratory cigar.

"Gentlemen," Luis proudly announced, "I just bagged a twelve-point buck with a single shot through the heart. Tonight we eat venison!"

Rob saw the curious look on Pedraza's face. His expression went beyond joy in the sport of hunting. The look suggested pleasure in the act of killing. It sent a chill down Rob's spine.

32

In the morning Rob took off on the Institute jet, leaving the magnificent Tetons behind. He had a lot to mull over during the flight back home. The anger he had when he first arrived in Jackson Hole had subsided. Given Jamison's word, he felt that he could move beyond the tragedy of Collier's death. Rob would work with Fleming on the clinical research protocols so there wouldn't be any more unforeseen surprises.

When he arrived back at the beach villa, Sarah greeted him.

"So, how'd it go?" she asked.

"As a matter of fact, I think things went pretty well. Jamison has quite a spread up in Wyoming. I did some fly-fishing. The scenery was spectacular."

"What about the issue of Fleming's research?"

"Well, Hal and I had a frank discussion, and he assured me there won't be a repeat of what occurred with Collier. He went on to tell me a lot more about the details of the Institute's current research program. Sarah, the prospects are staggering. If everything happens as he intends, I wouldn't be at all surprised if it leads to a Nobel Prize."

"Come on, Rob."

"Sarah, I'm serious. The work at the Institute is leading to the most significant advancements in transplant surgery since the field began. I guess I should count myself as fortunate to be here at ground zero witnessing a new era unfold before my eyes."

"Rob, when you left here, you were upset, so I'm glad you got things resolved. Now that you're back after a weekend of male bonding, perhaps you're ready for some bonding with me."

"What do you mean?" Rob said.

"Take me upstairs to the bedroom and find out." Sarah held her hand out for Rob. Gloria and Josh were away at the recreation center, and they were home all by themselves. Rob could feel himself stir in response to her unexpected invitation.

"Now that's an offer I can't refuse."

33

As soon as Rob left the lodge, Jamison phoned Fleming. "George, I want you to know there's no further need to worry about Sanders. Just do me one great favor. Tell him in advance about any experiments on his patients. And please make an effort to include him in the planning for our next project, the one with the primate organ donors. I don't think that should be too difficult, do you?"

"Look, Hal, Sanders is getting to be a big pain in the ass, but if that's what you want, so be it. The more important thing is that a batch of the newly modified Chimera Factor is cooking in the bioreactors as we speak. The pharmaceutical companies are practically fighting each other for the rights to the protein. There's no question in my mind the modified Chimera's structure will give us the ability to routinely do mammalian organ transplants in humans."

"George, I believe you, but let's not do something silly that would turn Sanders against us. Draft a research protocol for the project with a new consent form and go over the details with him. I'm sure he won't object to putting monkey kidneys in humans if we just do things by the book."

"I guess there is no harm in that," Fleming said.

Jamison went on. "By the way, I called Ricky and asked him to start easing Rob into our organ procurement program. Sanders will be more dedicated to our mission if he is involved in all our efforts."

With that, the conversation between the two men ended. Rob's initiation to organ procurement was about to begin.

Rob quickly returned to the pace of his busy surgical schedule at the Institute. The next few days flew by quickly. He even tackled the first dual kidney and pancreas transplant at the Institute, and his patient did well.

Rob was relaxing at home when he received a call from Ricky Pedraza.

"Say, tomorrow Jamison wants me to take you on one of our organ procurement runs. He wants you to get familiar with our setup. We leave at seven-thirty in the morning from the airfield, so please be on time. See you in the a.m."

The phone conversation ended so abruptly Rob didn't even have time to ask where they were flying. The transplant program at the Institute ran so smoothly Rob never questioned where the organs came from, assuming they originated from donors at other regional hospitals.

In the morning Rob went to the Institute airfield as requested. Don had brought along his Igloo containers. He was loading them into the storage area of the plane when Rob arrived.

"Good morning. Where are we off to?" Rob asked.

"Just going to one of our usual retrieval destinations. Come on, climb aboard."

Everybody got into the dual engine plane. Ricky sat in the pilot's seat, and Rob sat next to him. Adams sat in the back. The plane rumbled down the tarmac and became airborne, heading southwest. Rob observed, "Hey, we're going out over the ocean."

"That's right," Ricky chimed in. "We're en route to the *Ilas los Tres Marias,* the Islands of the Three Marias. The largest, Maria Madre, has a hospital on it. They call us when donors are available."

Rob had never heard of the islands and asked to look at the map. Ricky pulled out his navigation chart and pointed out the islands to Rob. "We'll be there in less than an hour," Ricky told him. "In the meantime, enjoy the view?" Rob put down the chart

and looked out the window. The blue waters below were punctuated by only an occasional whitecap. Mazatlan's great bay disappeared behind him. Finally, the islands came into view, looking
like three small dots floating on the horizon.

Ricky brought the plane down on a runway near the southwest corner of the largest island in the group. It bounced several
times before coming to a stop then taxied toward a building that
acted as the flight terminal for the island. Several men in khaki
fatigues approached the plane from the building. Rob could see
that each had a holster with a pistol strapped around the waist.
One carried a carbine.

"What is this place, an army base?" Rob asked

Ricky answered, *"No, mi amigo.* It's a penal colony."

34

Maria Madre had about fifteen hundred inmates. While island living might otherwise be idyllic, the accommodations were sparse and barely habitable. The inability to leave made the island what it was intended to be, a natural prison.

An SUV was waiting for them by the tarmac. As Ricky and Rob got into the vehicle, Don Adams took the Igloo containers from the plane and loaded them into the back. The guard who drove spent most of the ride telling jokes and making small talk with Ricky in Spanish. They traveled a few miles down a bumpy road then pulled off, heading to a building with a sign that read "*Infirmary Medico.*" Inside, Ricky introduced Sanders to the staff. "Please meet our new surgeon, Dr. Sanders, and be nice to him."

"Salvador Gutierrez," said one of the men who stepped up to say hello. He appeared to be in charge and spoke English. "Anything you need when you're here, you just tell me." Gutierrez turned to Ricky and said, "Your first two patients are waiting. Everything is prepared as usual."

Rob soon discovered that the infirmary had a fully equipped operating room with two surgical tables. After the three changed into surgical attire, only Adams and Ricky scrubbed at the sink located outside the operating room. Ricky told Rob, "Today I just want you to watch and see how we do things."

The trio entered the OR. Two patients were under general anesthesia, lying positioned on their sides, facing away from each other with their backs toward the center of the room. Pedraza went to one of the tables and Adams to the other. The patients had been prepped and draped by the staff. The operations began simultaneously, and within thirty-five minutes each surgeon had removed a kidney and placed it into an Igloo container. When the incisions were sutured up, the patients were repositioned on their backs and Rob saw their faces. One of the donors was male, the other female. Both were young, probably in their early twenties.

The entire operative procedure from skin to skin was done in a little over an hour. The unconscious patients were moved to a recovery area while two new patients were hurriedly set up for their procedures. Soon, the surgeons began to operate again. After they removed a kidney from one and a segment of liver from the other, Adams loaded the Igloos into the van. The procurement team changed and boarded for the ride to the airfield.

Before leaving Rob watched as Ricky reached into his briefcase and pulled out a thick manila envelope. He handed it to Gutierrez, who opened the envelope and looked inside. Rob saw that the envelope was stuffed with money.

Gutierrez smiled and said, "*Muchas gracias*, Dr. Ricky."

"Until next time, *compadre*," Pedraza replied.

At the airfield Adams loaded the coolers into the cargo hold of their plane. Ricky sat in the pilot's seat and buckled himself in. He started the engines. Within minutes, they were in the air, heading back to the mainland.

Ricky asked, "Rob, do you remember the old adage from your residency, 'see one, do one, teach one?' Well, you've just seen your first organ procurement on the island." Rob anticipated what was coming next. "Next time, you'll be the one who does the harvesting."

Rob remained silent. He had a bad feeling about what was just witnessed on Maria Madre.

Finally Rob spoke, "Ricky, those were obviously not cadaver kidneys you just took. Those were living donors."

"You're absolutely right. We prefer living donors because, as you know, their organs do better in the long run than cadaver material. While a kidney from a dead person is all right, the kidney of a living person is even better, and that means they go for a premium."

"What premium? You mean you pay the prisoners for their organ?"

"We pay Gutierrez, who acts as our agent, and makes all the arrangements. The persons who give us their kidney or segment of liver don't receive a single peso. Instead their sentences will be shortened. As soon as they recuperate from their surgery, they'll be released."

"Don't you consider that unethical?"

"Not in the least. The inmates on the island aren't tortured or forced to do this. They volunteer. What's more, for once they're doing something positive for society. What could be better than helping others who need a kidney or segment of liver to survive?"

"Ricky, letting prisoners out early if they become donors is a form of coercion. It's totally unethical."

"Rob, this is the system down here. Many people have been saved through our approach. Everyone is happy with the setup. The prisoner gets his freedom, the guards get some money, and sick patients get a new organ. What could be more ethical than that? I see no problem."

"What if a serious operative complication resulted in the death of a living donor? How could you justify it?"

"Rob, I told you, no one is holding a gun to their heads and making them to do this. Hell, when I was in Dallas, there was a group of religious zealots who each donated a kidney to someone they didn't even know."

"But in Dallas they weren't being paid off. They donated an organ out of the goodness of their hearts. Ricky, I don't feel right about what's going on here."

"Do you feel right about the patient on dialysis who dies while he is still waiting for a new kidney?"

"Well, of course not."

"Then think about it some more and you'll see it's actually a good system we've developed. Try to keep an open mind. Back in the States there are people lobbying to legalize the sale of organs as a means of increasing the availability for transplantation."

Rob's head was spinning. He remembered the case Hugo Iberra had told him about, a patient with a brain tumor who ran away rather than explain his missing kidney. The patient had said he was in prison in the past, but hadn't disclosed where he was held. It seemed plausible that he had once been an inmate on Maria Madre and had bought early release with his kidney.

After they landed at the Institute airfield, Don grabbed the coolers and took them back to the hospital. Ricky drove Rob home in his Porsche. As they drove, Rob remained silent, but his thoughts took him back to a comment made by his mentor when he spoke to him about a possible job at the Institute.

Rob could still hear Ryan's words, *"All that glitters isn't gold."* The glimmer of the Jamison Institute was quickly fading before Rob's eyes.

35

"**A**ll right, George," Jamison began, "can you summarize where we stand in our negotiations with the pharmaceutical companies?"

Fleming, Jamison, Hurley, and Luis Pedraza sat around a conference room table at the Institute. Together, they formed its board of directors.

George gave his report. "We have the following offers: ImmunoLogic; $200 million plus royalties of 6 percent on gross sales for four years. Adelphi BioPharma; $300 million plus 10 percent of the outstanding preferred stock. The class A currently trades for $24 a share on the New York Exchange. If the deal goes through, the stock price is likely to go up by at least 50 percent. That makes the deal worth as much as $600 million. Nashiki Pharmaceutical offered $400 million plus 3 percent royalty for the next five years."

Fleming paused for a moment, then continued with a smile. "Let me add this interesting bit of information. Based on the latest discussions, as soon as I can provide hard data that modified Chimera is effective in giving humans immune tolerance to organs from other mammals, the offers on the table could go up by 30 percent. I'm sure you can do the math in your heads. Not long from now, we may well be sitting on the better part of a billion-dollar deal!"

Jamison interjected, "Pat, you're a numbers person. What's your opinion on the offers?"

"I like the Adelphi deal best because it offers us a great base with the most upside. The company is a multi-billion-dollar operation growing at 15 percent annually. They also have an outstanding pipeline of new drugs on the horizon. Adelphi gets my vote."

Those sitting around the table acknowledged Pat's assessment, nodding in affirmation.

"Pat, can you update us on last quarter's financials here at the hospital?" Jamison inquired.

"Our last quarter was quite good, and I expect the present quarter will be even better. Since the addition of Dr. Sanders, the volume of surgical cases has gone up significantly. I expect to see an increase in both gross revenue and profit over the next few quarters. However, our margins decreased somewhat since we saw a rise in the cost of organ procurement. Net profit from operations for the last quarter was $6 million."

"Where did we see the increase in procurement costs?"

"The wardens at the jails in Tepic and Tijuana increased their fees significantly, and Gutierrez on the island is asking for more as well."

"Luis, you're responsible for the relationships with the wardens. Can you tell us what's going on?"

"Nothing that's unexpected. The wardens like to call it their cost of dying adjustment." Everyone chuckled.

Jamison spoke up, "Seriously, Luis, we just can't let our overhead spiral out of control."

"Hal, I totally agree with you. Don't forget, I'm the one who bankrolled the Institute being built in the first place. If anyone is interested in seeing more profit, it's me. Perhaps I don't have an MBA, but the way I see it, everything comes down to the simple principle of supply and demand. Those two factors determine the price of any commodity or service. Basically, the wardens know we depend on them as a major source for our transplant organs, so they jacked up the fee, and there's not much I can do about it. But I've been in contact with the penitentiary in Chiapas. With some alterations in their infirmary, it could accommodate an organ procurement setup. I know the warden there fairly well. He's ready and willing to cooperate with us. Another major source should put an end to the price increases."

Jamison asked, "Pat, what will a surgical setup at Chiapas end up costing us?"

"About $750 thousand for the kind of equipment we'll need to meet our requirements."

"That's a lot of money," Pedraza interjected.

Pat responded, "Well, let's put it in perspective. That's about what we collect for doing one heart transplant. The investment will pay for itself many times over in no time at all. Of course, all of this is an interim measure. When we start using animal donors, what we pay the wardens for the human organs will go down substantially."

Pedraza observed, "That's what I like about capitalism. Let free market principles operate, and it leads to the best financial results."

Pat continued, "There will always be clients who prefer to have a human organ rather than one from a pig or monkey, so we need to maintain relationships with our prison sources."

"Regarding timing," Fleming interjected, "our bioreactors are presently completing the cycle for production of newly modified Chimera Factor. Soon, the mammalian to human transplant program will be running at full throttle. It should take only a few months to accumulate enough cases to prove our point to the pharmaceutical companies."

"And collect our money," Pedraza interjected, smiling.

With the main issues discussed, Jamison was ready to call for a vote of the board members.

"Can I see a show of hands regarding moving ahead with the project at Chiapas? How many want to make the investment in setting up an operative suite there?" Everyone's hand shot up, including his own.

"The motion passes unanimously," Jamison announced, then he directed a request to Pedraza. "Luis, can you get the Chiapas deal finalized as soon as possible?"

"Consider it done," he answered.

Pat projected that the quarterly profit at the Institute would go up by $3 million once animal organs came into regular use. Pedraza kept all the numbers in his head. Louis was good at math for a man who hadn't finished high school. He had the ability to do the computations on his drug deals in his head as accurately as using a calculator. If the equation involved money, he could figure it out.

Pedraza sat contentedly at the table with the others. He would soon be an even richer and more powerful man. The medical business he had become involved with through his association with Jamison and Hurley was quite profitable, and all of Pat's financial projections pointed upward. The largest prize would soon be had when the deal for the rights to Chimera Factor was consummated, a deal that looked like it wasn't far off. Pedraza lit one of his cigars. He inhaled deeply then sent a series of smoke rings upward. So far, Luis liked the medical business. He liked it very much.

Luis's good relations with the prison wardens was borne out of the money he spent in getting his incarcerated gang members out from behind bars. Spreading cash among the wardens had made him their friend. It was relatively easy for them to make the adjustment and take money for finding inmate organ donors, while at the same time getting rid of the worst troublemakers at their facilities. Unlike the island, where they took only a kidney or a piece of liver and allowed the inmate to get an early release, at the penitentiaries the procurement team took all their organs. Afterward, the warden's men would dispose of the emptied corpse in an unmarked grave at the prison cemetery. The cause of death was usually listed as an accident or suicide.

The method by which inmates became organ donors for the Institute had become standardized. First, the prisoner was placed in solitary confinement. At the selected time, a dose of sedative was mixed with their meal. Once the inmate lost consciousness, he was dragged over to the jail infirmary, which had been converted to an operating room. Ricky and Don Adams would already have arrived by plane, along with their array of Igloo coolers in tow. The organ donor, made helpless by sedation, was then placed under general anesthesia. Ricky and Don would harvest every transplantable organ, not leaving anything behind that had potential value.

The 'ultimate donors,' as Ricky liked to call them, were worth a lot of money. Each lung would fetch $400, thousand, the heart $750 thousand, the liver $500 thousand, a pancreas $400 thousand, and each kidney $250 thousand. Transplanting all those organs from a single person could bring in close to $3 million dollars to the Institute. It was easy to see why Ricky preferred making the trip to a penitentiary or the white building in the desert rather than the island penal colony on Maria Madre. At Maria Madre they would fly back with only a few kidneys and possibly a segment of liver. Like his father, Ricky had a business mentality. He liked to make the most money in the shortest time and that meant operating to take every possible organ from the donor.

As the meeting of the board ended, Jamison went to his office and put a call in for Ricky. Regarding handling the situation with Rob, Jamison's instructions to him were quite clear. Ricky was to ease Rob into taking part in organ procurement. Hal told him, "Take it slow with Sanders. We don't want a repeat of Wes O'Brien."

Ricky's new colleague certainly wasn't ready to visit the penitentiaries right off the bat. Instead, he would initiate Sanders at the island. At least on Maria Madre the inmates left the operating room alive and that shouldn't be difficult for Sanders to handle. Once he was sure Sanders was comfortable doing organ retrieval on the island, Ricky would advance him to operating on ultimate donors at the white building or penitentiaries. Pedraza could hardly wait to have Rob share the load of organ procurement, especially the cases that came up unexpectedly. Since Rob was a junior associate, he would soon be the one to whom Ricky could punt cases when they didn't suit his schedule. Just the thought of it put a smile on Ricky's face.

36

arah was on the cellphone with her mother when Rob walked though the door. The phone bills were going to be big, but at least now they could afford them. Having turned down an opportunity at the Cleveland Clinic barely two hundred miles from her parents' home, she felt a greater need to stay in close touch with them by phone. Sarah turned to Rob. "Mom and Dad say hello. Dad thinks they might be able to fly his plane down sometime next month."

"Say hi from me, and tell them I look forward to their visit."

Sarah noticed that Rob looked upset.

"Rob, dinner is on the table, I'll join you in a minute."

He didn't have much of an appetite after what had transpired on Maria Madre. When Sarah finished the phone call, she joined him in the kitchen.

"What's wrong, Rob?"

"There are some things going on besides Fleming's research that I don't like."

"Can you tell me about it?"

"Today I visited a place where the Institute gets some of its organ donor material. It's not a hospital. It's a prison on an island about one hour's flight by plane. I wouldn't have believed it, except I saw it for myself. An inmate who gives up a kidney or portion of liver gets a reduced sentence. I saw Pedraza hand one of the guards an envelope filled with money. For Ricky, paying off the guards and harvesting inmate organs is simply business as usual, but I don't want to have any part in it."

"Rob, what you're telling me is disturbing. You need to let Jamison know about it."

"I'm not sure that would help. He seems so totally committed to his vision of building the world's premier transplant hospital that I think he's lost sight of the ethical issues. I remember reading an article about the sale of organs in India, Pakistan, and China, but now I find myself caught up in something just as bad right here at the Institute."

"Listen," Sarah said to him, "if this place isn't right for you, we'll pack up and go somewhere else. Why don't you tell Jamison you don't want to remove organs from prison inmates? If he wants you to stay on at the Institute, he'll accommodate your wishes."

"You're probably right, but I have to wonder about working in a place where everybody else has a different standard. I've got to give Hugo Iberra a call and see what he thinks. He's about the only person down here I feel I can trust."

Rob went to bed that night but couldn't sleep. He spent the night staring at the ceiling, tossing and turning as he thought about what his next move should be.

Rob stood across a surgical table from Ricky, while he was doing a liver transplant. After the abdomen was opened, Rob saw that the patient's liver looked perfectly healthy instead of being the small, scarred organ that the typical cirrhotic liver looked like. Rob didn't want to remove the healthy-looking liver.

"Hey, this liver is perfectly normal. There must be some mistake. I can't just remove a healthy liver."

Ricky started laughing. Rob was confused then felt a stinging sensation in his arm. He turned and saw Don injecting him with a syringe. Rob suddenly felt dizzy, and the room began spinning as he lost consciousness.

When his eyes opened, he was lying on his back looking up at a bank of operative lights. Ricky and Don's faces were directly above him. Rob's arms and legs were strapped to the table.

"What's going on?" Rob asked. Ricky bent down to whisper in Rob's ear.

"*Mi Amigo,* the time has come for you to donate your organs."

Ricky wasn't wearing a surgical mask or gloves. Instead, he was dressed in his street clothes with his shirtsleeves rolled up.

"Give me the saw," Ricky ordered. Rob could see the glare of light reflecting from the blade's surface. Ricky turned the switch on, and a high-pitched whine began. He slowly brought the saw's blade down toward Rob's chest.

As Rob felt the touch of the cold metal on his skin, he screamed, "Stop! No. No!"

Rob awoke from sleep drenched in sweat. He placed his hand on his chest and felt reassured it was still intact. His thrashing had roused Sarah from her sleep.

"Rob, what's wrong?" she asked.

"It's just a bad dream." But even as Rob tried to forget his frightening dream, he realized it meant something had to change. He knew he simply couldn't go on working at the Institute any longer.

37

Hugo was home when the phone rang. "Dr. Iberra, it's Rob Sanders from the Institute. Do you have a moment?"

"Sure, Rob, what is it?"

"I think I may have an answer regarding your patient with the brain tumor and the missing kidney, the one who left before his surgery."

"Yes, please tell me."

"The other day I flew to an island called Maria Madre. It's off the coast about one hundred miles south of here, and it's a penal colony. While I was there, I witnessed surgery on two people, a man and a woman, each of who had a kidney removed. On the island an organ donation gets the inmate a reduced prison sentence, and the guards who work there get money from the Institute.

Hugo, I believe your patient was once a prisoner on the island. He gave a kidney for his freedom, but was told to keep his mouth shut."

"You know, Rob, that wouldn't surprise me. Jamison and your colleagues at the Institute have only one thing on their mind—money. Organ transplant is just a means to their end of getting rich. I don't think human rights or, for that matter, human life matters much to them."

"But what do I say when they tell me they aren't doing anything against the law, that the system is purely voluntary?"

"Rob, it can't be legal for officials to take money and let inmates have their sentences commuted. If what you're telling me was made known to certain authorities, it might be possible to put an end to this practice. Let me make some inquiries among people I trust. In the meantime, play along and learn as much as you can without jeopardizing your own safety."

The next day at the Institute, Rob met with Jamison and raised the issue of procuring organs from inmates on Maria Madre. Rather than get upset, Hal answered in a calm voice.

"Rob, that's just the way things are done down here. There's no official organ procurement program south of Texas, so we had to come up with one of our own. If you feel uncomfortable about it, I can respect that. I'll talk to Ricky. He might be able to make arrangements so you don't have to do procurement."

"You will?"

"Sure, if that'll make you happy," Jamison answered.

Rob planned to resign from the Institute if things weren't changed to his liking. It would be a shame for him and his family to leave a place that until now had been like paradise. Rob was glad that Jamison understood his position and was willing to make an accommodation. Maybe things would work out after all.

For his part, Jamison remained confident Rob would come to the same conclusion he had years before, that in order to save the lives of many, a few might have to be sacrificed. He didn't lose any sleep over the hardened criminals whose organs were removed. If some people died while Fleming conducted his research medical practice was changed for the better then that was just fine. Jamison knew one day Rob would share his philosophy.

38

A week had passed since Rob's flight to the penal colony and his last conversation with Iberra. Things settled back into a routine until early one morning he was awakened by someone knocking at the front door. Rob ran downstairs and found it was Don Adams at the doorway.

"Listen, Rob, I need you right away. I can't get hold of Ricky, and a donor needs to be harvested as soon as possible."

"Sure," Rob said while still half asleep. "Just give me a second to get ready." Rob threw on some clothes and went outside. He climbed into the passenger seat of Don's van. They took off speeding with a full complement of Igloo coolers in the back.

"Where are we flying to?" Rob asked.

"No, this time we don't need to fly. We're not going that far at all, maybe fifteen miles outside of town."

Rob was surprised. He had no idea there was any medical facility located in the heart of the desert.

When the van arrived at the compound, the guard allowed them to enter, and Don drove up to a white building at the center of the complex.

"What are we doing here?" Rob asked.

Don explained, "This is one of our organ procurement centers. There are people in Mazatlan who consider it sacrilegious to remove organs from dead bodies and try to make trouble for us. So we like to keep things quiet about organ retrieval. This place in the desert avoids public exposure."

Rob followed Adams inside.

"Come, let's go change." Rob followed Don into the locker room. They put on surgical attire and scrubbed at the sink outside the OR. Entering the room, Rob saw a body lying on the surgical table with an intravenous infusion running full blast. The patient was already hooked up to a ventilator. Rob couldn't see his face, which was covered by the surgical drape. They began the procedure. Adams informed him that all the organs were slated for harvesting. In just over an hour and a half, they were through. The kidneys, lungs, pancreas, and heart were placed into their respective coolers. Rob did the surgery, and Don assisted. He wondered about the cause of death.

As he moved back from the operating table Rob's shoe stepped into a pool of blood on the floor. *That's strange,* he thought. *We didn't lose any blood during the procedure.*

Rob pulled off his surgical gloves and his gown. Out of curiosity he decided to look above the barrier that hid the patient's face. What he saw shocked him. It was the face of a man in his twenties who had a gaping hole on the left side of his head dripping blood onto the floor. He noticed a small hole was on his right temple with a surrounding burn mark. Rob didn't have to be a forensic pathologist to know what happened. The patient had been killed by a single shot to the head at close range.

Rob drew the obvious conclusion. The person lying on the operating table was alive when he arrived at the compound, otherwise he would have bled so much on his way his organs would be unfit for procurement. That could only mean one thing—the man had been murdered at the compound just before he and Adams arrived.

Adams knew the details about the dead man, Caesar Ramirez, a local drug dealer whose business was dwarfed by that of Luis Pedraza. Luis tolerated Ramirez since he paid him a percentage of sales. However, like many before him, Caesar got greedy and tried expanding his business without permission.

When word got back to Luis, it brought a swift response. Early that morning Hector and Ramon woke him up. Ramon told him, "You need to come to a breakfast meeting with the *patron*."

"Meeting about what?" Ramirez asked.

"Hell if I know, but the *patron* insists that you come."

Caesar came along peaceably, and they drove him to the white building. Ramirez was worth much more dead than alive. His organs would fetch over one million dollars in fees from the clients who came to the Institute for a transplant.

Rob froze, and he didn't move from where he stood, his eyes transfixed on the patient's face. "Let's get going, Rob, our job is done and we have to leave," Adams said.

Rob realized the man was brain dead before he began the surgery, but it made him sick to think he had removed the organs from someone who was murdered only a short time before. Don was right; he had to go, and now there was no doubt about it. Rob had to leave the Institute, the sooner, the better.

In the van on the way back to the hospital Rob was silent. Don sensed something wasn't right and began the conversation.

"Rob, I appreciate you helping me out of this jam. Ricky will catch hell from Jamison for not being available. Mazatlan isn't all that big, but no one seems to know where Ricky is, and he wasn't answering his phone or beeper. I've been working here for years, and nothing like this has happened before. I hope I didn't cause too much of a stir over at your house so early in the morning."

Don sounded so sincere, yet he had to be deeply involved in the Institute's blatantly criminal activities. It shocked Rob that his work on Maria Madre and at the desert facility didn't disturb Adam's conscience.

"Don, how did you get involved in this business? Didn't you realize the man in there was murdered just before we arrived?"

"Look, Rob, it's really simple. When I started working here, I decided not to think about what I get paid to do. I'm better off that way, and you would be too. The last thing you want to do is interfere with the way things are done around here. Think about that." Don paused for a moment then went on. "At least when some lowlife hood is taken out, they don't go to waste. For once, these scumbags are making a contribution that will benefit society. Hell, recycling their body parts makes perfect sense to me."

"Don, can't you see that what you're doing is wrong? There's no justification for murdering someone."

"Hey, Dr. Sanders, like I said, I don't make the rules down here. I just do my job. You can see what happens to people who make trouble for Luis Pedraza. They get recycled. I'm just a worker bee who's trying to make a living. If I didn't do the work for Jamison, he'd just find someone else. No rocking the boat for me."

Rob was floored by Don's response and realized he wouldn't support a rebellion against the Institute's practices.

"I see your point," Rob responded. "Do you know anyone else who has a problem with what they are doing down here? There are a lot of other doctors on the staff of the hospital."

"I don't like to talk about things like that."

"Come on, Don, I'll keep it between us."

"Promise me you'll keep it between us."

"Sure," Rob replied.

"Well, about a year ago we had a transplant surgeon come from Seattle. Nice guy about your age, and he was real good in the OR. He wasn't down here very long when he started having arguments with Jamison. Once I saw him in a shouting match with Pat Hurley. After that, things got a bit ugly. Anyway, he left after that. Moved back to Seattle where his family was from. Other than that, things here have been running pretty smoothly."

"Do you remember his name?"

"I think his name was Wes...yes, Dr. Wesley O'Brien."

Don pulled up the villa's driveway. As Rob stepped from the van, Don called out, "Just our secret about Dr. O'Brien?"

"Sure, Don, it's just our little secret."

Adams drove off to the hospital and logged the harvested organs in at the depository. Over the next few days and weeks all of Caesar's vital organs would eventually find a new home in an Institute patient.

The following morning it was almost eight-thirty and Rob needed to shower and shave before leaving for work at the hospital. He began to think about how he was going to extricate himself from the Jamison Institute.

Before leaving for the hospital, there was one more thing he wanted to do. He made a phone call to Seattle. He wanted to speak with Wes O'Brien. He called the Department of Surgery office at University Hospital, but was told Wes O'Brien's name wasn't among the active staff members. Records in the department of surgery showed that Dr. O'Brien had taken a position at the Jamison Institute about two years before. As far as they could tell, he was still there. Rob thanked them and hung up.

Adams had told Rob that O'Brien had family in Seattle. Rob called information and took down the numbers of persons with the last name O'Brien. Luckily, the second phone number on his list belonged to Wes's mother. Rob told her he was a transplant surgeon who worked at the Jamison Institute. Then he politely asked, "I have to get in touch with your son right away. Do you know where I can reach him?"

"I can't believe you're calling to talk with Wes. Don't you know about the accident?"

"I'm sorry, what accident?"

"Wes drowned in a boating accident off the coast of Mazatlan a year ago. They never found his body."

"Oh, I'm so sorry," Rob responded, "I had no idea."

Rob got off the phone, trembling. From what Adams had told him it seemed likely O'Brien had made enemies of Jamison and Hurley by standing up against the Institute's practices and paid for it with his life. Rob had to be cautious. If he made the wrong move now he could also end up the victim of an accident.

39

As instructed, Don called Ricky on his cell as soon as he finished processing the organs from the desert compound. Ricky asked, "So, how did it go out there with Sanders?"

"I'm not sure," Don answered. "He seemed fine at first, but on the way back he started talking about ethics and wondering how I got involved."

"You know something, I warned Jamison about this guy. Sanders seemed too independent for my taste, but Hal was sure he'd come around. I don't know why he was so hot for him to join us. Maybe it was just because Sanders came from the same place he did in Boston. 'Ease him into organ procurement; he'll turn into the most devoted supporter of our program.' Bullshit!

"Jorge told me he's had a meeting with Hugo Iberra. Remember when Iberra and his friend the coroner tried to implicate the Institute for the empty corpse in the desert? Well, if it wasn't for the shitload of money my father gave the police, we would have been up to our necks in an investigation that could have ruined everything."

Adams interjected, "Why don't we give it a little more time to see how things play out? We can always figure out a way to get rid of him if we have to, but he's a damn good surgeon and I'd hate to lose another good set of hands. Maybe Jamison is right, and Sanders will settle down."

Ricky spoke up, "We gave him plenty of money, a villa by the ocean and a new car. He should have shown some gratitude instead of questioning everything. Where the hell else does he think he could live like a king as a new associate?"

Don added, "Let's hope he comes around."

Ricky concluded, "You know, if Jamison was really smart, he'd just stick to the research and surgery and leave the hiring and management up to me."

When Rob returned home from the hospital later that day, he told Sarah everything. He told her that there was no way he could continue working there after what he encountered in the desert. He had to leave.

"Sarah, I don't care about the salary or the house. Jamison can have it all back. We've got to leave this place as soon as possible."

The whole thing made Rob sick, and the more he thought about it, the more urgent was his desire to go. "Sarah, I hate to do this to you and Josh on such short notice, but we need to start packing our things. Try to get us out on the earliest flight you can find back to the States." Rob went upstairs and wrote a letter of resignation.

Early the next morning, Rob got into the Land Rover, put his letter on the passenger seat, and headed in the direction of Jamison's estate. He planned to catch Hal before he left for work. Rob pulled up to the front gate and pressed the buzzer. He heard the voice of Pat Hurley over the intercom.

"Rob, what a pleasant surprise, I'll let you in." The gate opened and Rob drove in.

He walked up the same path he took with Sarah when they first met Jamison and Hurley, then he let himself into the house. No one was there.

"Hellooo?" Rob called out, announcing his presence to the empty foyer.

"I'm in the study," Pat's voice returned from the distance.

Rob made his way down the hall to the room where he found Hurley sitting in a bathrobe behind Jamison's massive desk.

Pat looked down at the robe she was wearing and said, "I must apologize for my attire, but I hardly expected a visitor at this hour. What brings you here so early?"

Rob answered, "I wanted to catch Hal before he left for work."

"Sorry, Rob, but he left about a half-hour ago. Can I help you?"

"I needed to tell him something important, but I wanted to speak with him personally."

"Rob, you sound upset. Is something bothering you?"

Rob hesitated for a moment then spoke. "Well, I suppose it's only right that I tell you. After all, you were the one who hired me. I've decided to leave the Institute. In fact, I have a letter of resignation with me." He placed the envelope on the desk in front of Hurley.

She opened the letter and read its curt message:

Dear Dr. Jamison,

Effective immediately, I resign from the staff of the Institute.

Rob Sanders M.D.

Pat responded, "You must be kidding, Rob. You can't be serious about leaving?"

"To the contrary, I couldn't be more serious."

Hurley was dumbfounded. "Let me understand," she said. "You've been given everything anyone could possibly want and you want to quit?" She paused briefly then continued. "Perhaps the workload has gotten to you? Maybe you need some time off. Here, let me go make you a drink."

She started to get up from the chair but Rob interjected, "Pat, don't bother getting up. I don't need a drink."

She thought for a moment then made another suggestion. "Well, maybe I can offer something else." Provocatively, she undid her bathrobe and allowed it to slide off her shoulders, exposing her breasts. In a seductive voice she said, "Rob, it's just the two of us here. Let's go to the bedroom and enjoy each other."

Rob was unmoved. "Look," he said, "you just don't get it. I'm done with the Institute. I've had enough of the crap that's going on around here. I resign!"

"You resign," Pat sarcastically echoed, as she readjusted the bathrobe to cover herself. "You can't just up and leave on such short notice. It's unacceptable. It's impossible."

"I'm sorry, but my family and I will be on the next flight out of Mazatlan that's heading for the States."

"Rob, Dr. Jamison won't stand for this!"

"Pat, I've made my mind up. I can't continue implanting organs that come from prisoners or victims of murder. This is a far cry from what I had in mind when I came down here to work."

"But, Rob, this is *Mazatlan,* not Boston, and things are different here."

"It doesn't matter where we are. It's a straightforward issue. What's going on here is just plain wrong."

Pat lowered her tone and tried to make a rational plea.

"Look, Rob, think about it. You also have a family to consider, and I'm not sure I can guarantee their safety if you try to leave now. Around here, people sometimes disappear."

"You mean like Wes O'Brien?" Rob retorted

"How did you know about O'Brien?"

"It doesn't matter. What matters is that I'm through working for you and the Institute."

"Rob, are you absolutely sure about what you're saying?"

"Yes, I'm absolutely sure."

"In that case, let me make another point." Pat rose from her chair, opened a drawer of the desk, and pulled out a gun.

"Rob, Jamison thinks the world of you. You're a talented surgeon. Don't throw it all away. We can make it worth your while to stay. You could be the highest-paid junior associate in the history of surgery. Just tell me you'll stay and forget this moralistic nonsense."

"I can't forget about it. What's happening here goes against everything I believe in."

Rob was slowly backing up, trying to increase the distance between them.

"Rob, think. We've solved the main problem that has plagued organ transplantation since the field began. Imagine, unlimited transplants using organs from other species and no rejection. The benefit to mankind is unfathomable and so will be the financial reward for us. Couldn't you try to go with the flow a little longer?"

"Pat, I'm sorry you can't see how twisted this place has become, but I'm done with it."

She pointed her gun at him. "You just stand where you are while I make a phone call. I'll shoot if I have to. And don't you think for a second I'm upset because you didn't want to fuck me. That's got nothing to do with it. I put my heart and soul into making the Institute a success, and I'm not about to let you do anything that will jeopardize it." Hurley picked up the phone on the desk and started dialing. When someone answered at the other end she said, "Can you get Ricky for me?"

Realizing he had to act quickly, Rob glanced to his side and saw the loaded crossbow hanging on the wall next to him. He grabbed it off the mounting and sprinted back toward the door.

Behind him, Rob heard her yell, "Shit!" A gunshot rang out. He felt pressure on the side of his right thigh as he ran out the doorway of the study and toward the front entry. Pat threw the phone down and was trying to run after him from behind the desk, but was held up as she tripped over her robe. By the time she reached the study's entrance, Rob had already exited the front door and run into the garden alcove. Birds disturbed by the sudden commotion flew in every direction.

Rob headed off the path, looking for a place to hide. He saw a banyan tree to his left and made for it. He stood still behind one of its larger trunks while his heart pounded and beads of perspiration formed on his forehead. He felt something wet on his leg and looked down to see his pants soaked in blood. It wasn't a fatal injury, but he would weaken from blood loss if he didn't attend to the wound. He took his belt off and tightened it around his upper thigh as a makeshift tourniquet.

As Pat exited the front of the house, she stopped and listened for any sound of movement. The birds had quieted, and all was silent. Then, she noted spatters of blood leading away from the house.

"Rob, you're injured, but it's not too late to make a deal. We'll get you patched up like nothing happened. No one else has to know about this but you and I. Come on, Rob, be reasonable."

He saw from behind the tree that she was less than fifty feet away walking slowly with the gun in her hand. Pat intermittently looked down at the ground as she followed his blood trail.

Rob thought about Sarah and Josh. Their lives were at risk. Sarah knew about the dealings of the Institute, and they would never let her go once they found out. It was hopeless to think of reasoning with Hurley. She would surely kill him if she had another chance.

Rob had no intention of becoming an involuntary organ donor for the Institute. He undid the safety on the crossbow's trigger. Pat was less than thirty feet away when Rob picked up a stone and threw it toward a clump of bushes to his side. Birds flew out startling Pat. She turned and fired several rounds at the bush. Rob had only one chance to save himself. There was only one arrow in the crossbow. He held the bow steady and emerged from behind the Banyan. He called out, "Pat, you bitch, I'm over here!"

As Hurley turned to face him, Rob pulled the trigger and released the arrow. The eighteen-inch-long metal shaft with its sharp steel-tipped head flew forward. The force of the blow pushed Hurley backward nearly lifting her off the ground as the arrow penetrated her chest. The arrow's tip lodged into the base of a palm tree behind her, pinning her upright. The gun fell from her hand to the ground. She tried to reach for the gun, but it was impossible to bend forward. Pat stared at Rob with eyes wide open, unable to produce a sound. She frantically tried pulling at the segment of arrow protruding from her chest, but it wouldn't budge. Moments later Pat's body went limp, and her head fell forward. Pat Hurley was dead.

No longer needing to escape his attacker, Rob shifted focus to his own condition. He dropped the discharged crossbow and felt a searing pain in his right thigh as he tried to walk. Rob fell to his knees as his legs buckled. He grabbed a branch on the ground and used it as a cane, walking back to the house. Inside, he went to Jamison's study. Rob couldn't call for medical assistance since that would be signing his own death warrant. Instead, he called Sarah on her cell.

"Sarah, where are you?"

"I'm at the villa."

"Listen, we have to get out of here immediately. I've been shot by Pat Hurley."

"What? Are you badly hurt?"

"I'll be fine, but they're going to kill all of us if they catch us. Have Gloria take you and Josh in her car and drive to the city. Go to the municipal hospital and page Dr. Iberra. Tell him who you are and that there's an emergency that requires his help. I'll connect with you later. There are a few things I have to do before leaving."

"Rob, please be careful. Should I call the police for help?"

"I'm not sure we can trust the police."

"Rob, please promise to call me as soon as you can."

"I love you, Sarah."

Rob couldn't get it out of his mind that he had just killed someone, even if it was someone as evil as Pat Hurley. Once Ricky found out what happened, the whole city would be looking for them. With Pedraza's gang of thugs, his life and the lives of Sarah and Josh were in the balance.

Rob limped over to the liquor cabinet and pulled out a bottle of whisky. Next, going to the worktable where Jamison made his lures, he picked up a hemostat and scissors, dousing them with liquor. He opened one of the suture packets that Jamison had on the table. Tearing open his pants in the area where the bullet entered to better expose his wound he poured the whisky over the bullet hole. Finally, Rob chugged a few gulps down to act as pain killer. At the moment there weren't many things to be thankful for, but he was certainly glad the bullet missed his femoral artery.

Rob probed into the bullet hole with a hemostat and the pain caused him to bite hard on his lower lip. He felt the tip of the instrument contact metal, opened its teeth and engaged the slug, pulling it from his thigh. With the bullet out, he took suture and started sewing the wound closed. It wasn't an operating room, but with the implements Jamison used to make his fish flies, Rob was able to do a reasonable closure.

Rob picked up Hurley's ID card and keys from the desk. He wanted to escape, but felt he had to try and put an end to the Institute. What Rob needed was solid evidence he could take to authorities other than the local police. It would be risky, but he had to go back.

40

Rob exchanged his bloody slacks for a pair of scrubs he found in Jamison's closet. He limped out of the house to the spot where Hurley's lifeless body stood pinned to the tree. He bent down and picked up her gun from the ground. *Just in case,* he thought, tucking it in at his waistline. He left his shirt hanging out to hide the gun. Getting into the Land Rover, Rob sped off to the Institute hospital. He parked in the doctor's lot and limped into the building, heading for the organ depository.

Hal Jamison had brought Rob there on his initial tour of the hospital. He recalled how Jamison had proudly shown off the collection of donor organs in their perfusion tanks. The depository was located at the far end of the hall past the operating rooms. Entry was restricted.

It was a chancy move, but he had to take the risk. If there was evidence to be had, it resided in that room. Rob had Hurley's ID card in his pocket. He gambled that it would be able to gain access to any area in the facility, but he wouldn't know for sure until he tried.

He passed a surgical nurse on his way to the operating room area. "Good morning, Dr. Sanders. Did you hurt your leg? You're limping."

"Just slipped and twisted my ankle getting out of the pool this morning."

"That's too bad. I hope it's better soon. But no doctor would recommend standing on a severely sprained ankle for hours while performing an operation. You should go home, get off your feet and give it a rest."

"You're probably right. I'll tell Jamison I need to take the day off."

"I'll tell him for you if you like."

"No, that's all right. Which room is he in?"

The nurse glanced over to the schedule board.

"Dr. Jamison is in OR three, doing a pancreas."

Rob pushed open the door and entered the operating room. Jamison looked up from the operative field to address him. "Say, Rob, what happened? We were expecting you much earlier."

"I slipped and twisted my ankle by the pool. I thought it would be fine, but it's getting worse by the minute and starting to swell."

"You think you broke something?"

"No. I'm not an orthopedic surgeon, but I don't think I'd be able to stand on it if something was broken. It's probably just a bad sprain."

"Well, pick up some pain killers at the pharmacy, go home and stick an ice pack on your ankle. I need you better by tomorrow, because the schedule is booked solid with cases. Ricky and Don are supposed to do organ procurement so there won't be anybody else around to help out but you."

"I'll see you tomorrow, even if I have to use crutches." Rob lied. He left the operating room, but instead of heading in the direction of the doctor's lounge he walked to the far end of the hallway. He approached a door marked "Organ Depository." He took out Hurley's ID card from his pocket and swiped the security panel.

His gamble worked. The door's lock clicked open, and Rob entered the frigid room. He was surrounded by glass tanks arranged on the shelves containing hearts, lungs, kidneys, and pancreases. Each tank had a label indicating the organ inside and time of arrival. Rob wasn't thinking of taking any of the organs with him. Without the body it came from, it wouldn't prove anything. He had something else in mind. He wanted to find the logbooks.

There was a desk in the far corner of the room and a number of journals were located on a shelf above it. He walked over, picked one of them and began scanning the pages. It contained meticulous records regarding the origin of donor tissues. Among the many entries, he found what he was looking for:

Case 346: Wesley O'Brien

Organs Deposited: heart, lungs, pancreas, liver, kidneys

Arrival date: 11/22/12

Rob had never met his predecessor, but the thought of his life being reduced to the organs listed in the log made him furious. If it was the last thing he did, Rob vowed to bring the barbaric practices of the Institute to an end.

He took the logbook and exited the frigid room. He walked back down the hall past the doctor's locker room, and just as he was about to leave he realized he had forgotten something. Perhaps it was crazy, but he went into the locker room. Ricky Pedraza walked out of a shower with a towel around his waist. He spotted Rob.

"What happened?" Ricky asked. "You didn't show this morning so I had to do your case."

"Sorry, Ricky, but I slipped and twisted the hell out of my ankle after my morning swim. Got here late, and Hal took pity on me. He told me to go home and ice it. I'll be back first thing tomorrow."

"Well, I guess shit happens. Hope the ankle is better by tomorrow because there's a full surgical schedule. Adams and I have to harvest some organs so your services will be needed here."

Rob reassured him, "I'm sure I'll be good as new by the morning."

Ricky took out a razor from his locker and walked back into the shower area to shave. Rob opened his own locker and reached in to take the only thing of value he wanted to bring back with to the States. He grabbed the box containing the Zeiss lenses, which were a gift from Dr. Ryan. Rob closed his locker then left the Institute hospital for the last time.

Rob got into his Land Rover and drove off. No one was home when he arrived at the beach villa. He hobbled upstairs and changed into street clothes. He went to the medicine cabinet, took out a bottle of antibiotic capsules, and, after swallowing two of them, put several more in his pocket. The conditions of the surgery he had performed on his leg were less than ideal. It wouldn't hurt to take some antibiotics and prevent an infection from setting in.

Rob went down to the kitchen and phoned Sarah on her cell. He was glad to hear that Gloria was able to take her and Josh to the city hospital.

"We're fine, Rob, don't worry. Dr. Iberra is with us, and he wants to talk to you."

"Go ahead, put him on the line."

"Rob, Sarah has briefed me on what has happened. Let me tell you what you probably already know, that all of you are in grave danger. Luis Pedraza and his son Ricky don't fool around. Crossing them is usually a death sentence. They will have men all over the city looking for you the moment they get the order. We must think quickly and decide what to do."

Sarah spoke up in the background, "Dr. Iberra, I think I have an idea. Can I speak with Rob?" Hugo handed the phone over to Sarah.

"Brilliant!" Rob said after Sarah related her plan of escape. His spirits were lifted by her ingenious idea in spite of the fact he knew they would soon be hunted by a vicious gang of thugs.

Pedraza would quickly mobilize his forces to shut down every exit from the city. The airport would be blanketed with his men and every departing flight closely watched. Even leaving by boat wouldn't work, since the harbor would undoubtedly be under surveillance as well.

However, if Sarah was correct, there was a way of getting out of Mazatlan that would be totally unexpected. "Rob, I'm going to call my father. Remember when he flew into Chicago in the business jet with his friend Clay? Maybe he can fly down here and get us."

"But Pedraza's men will be all over the airport."

"They'll be at the Mazatlan airport, thinking we'd take a commercial flight, but not at the Institute airfield."

Rob thought about it for a moment and drew the same conclusion. "You're right. They'd never expect us to get picked up in our own private jet. Never in a million years! Call your dad, and let's pray that he'll be able to help us."

Sarah dialed her father's cell number and let it ring, but there was no answer until the voice mail came on. She left her short message. When her father listened to it, the sound of desperation in her voice would be obvious. "Dad, there's an emergency down here in Mexico. You have to call me on my cell as soon as you can. I'm waiting to hear from you."

Hugo Iberra was thinking as Sarah made her phone call, *Where can I hide these two in case Pedraza's men come looking for them here?* Then, he thought of one place in the hospital that might be a safe place for them, the morgue.

Sarah's phone rang. It was her father.

"What's the matter, honey?" He asked. "You sounded upset in your message."

"Dad, we have a big problem. Rob found out the Institute has been getting most of its donor organs by murdering people. Jamison, the doctor who runs the place, is partners with a local drug lord who wants to prevent us from leaving alive. Rob has been shot, but managed to escape. We need to get out, but every route will be watched. But, there's a private airfield that the Institute owns, and I think it might offer a way out if you can find someone to come and get us."

"Sweetheart, don't worry. I'll phone Clay. We'll fly to Mazatlan in his jet. At five hundred miles an hour and a single stop for refueling, I imagine we'll arrive some time between four and five o'clock in the morning your time."

"We'll be waiting for you at the airfield."

"How is Josh doing?"

"Josh is fine. Dad, this might be dangerous. These guys will use their guns without thinking twice."

"Don't worry. Clay and I will be packing our own firepower. We've been through some tough spots together. This won't be so bad. Anyway, just make sure you're at the airfield on time, and we'll take care of the rest."

"Love you, Daddy," she said, then hung up.

Rob was wondering how to join his family at the hospital without being found out. His Land Rover was large and conspicuous. If he parked it anywhere near the hospital someone would likely spot it and realize he was there. Then, it wouldn't be long before he was captured. Instead, he decided to drive to Gloria's house and seek her assistance. He prayed she would say yes when he asked her to drive him to the public hospital.

41

H al Jamison pulled up the driveway to his home at 4 p.m. It struck him as odd that Pat hadn't answered his calls. No one had seen her come in to the hospital that morning. *Probably stayed home to finish something she was doing on the computer when I left,* he thought as he walked up the path to his front door. When he saw blood spots he slowed his pace, wondering what had happened. Rather than enter his house, he followed the blood trail off the path.

Seeing Pat's body, Jamison stopped dead in his tracks. He prayed his eyes were deceiving him. She was positioned upright against the tree trunk with her head bowed over and her limbs hanging limp. Her skin was ashen gray and the bathrobe, which had come undone from her final thrashing, revealed blood covering her exposed breasts and chest. The hunting arrow had penetrated to its terminal portion, marked by three yellow feathers.

Jamison was aghast. Pat Hurley had been with him from the beginning. She was the only human being for whom he felt anything approaching love, and now Pat was dead. Hal Jamison did something he hadn't done for a long time. He began to cry.

With tears streaming down his face, Hal left her pinned against the palm and walked like a zombie into the house. He went to his study and sat in the chair at his desk. The side drawer was open, and he noticed his gun was gone. He saw a letter lying on his desk and picked it up. As he read the short note he understood exactly what had happened.

Jamison screamed, "Sanders, you fucking son of a bitch!" and his curse reverberated through the mansion.

Anger suddenly thrust Jamison back into reality. He picked up the telephone and called Ricky.

"Ricky, I left the hospital and came home. I found her dead!"

"Hal, what the hell are you talking about?"

"Pat...Pat, she's been murdered. I found a letter of resignation Sanders wrote lying on the desk in my study. He must have stopped by to tell me, but I'd already left, and they got into a fight. Sanders killed her!"

"Hal, I had a bad feeling about that guy from day one."

"Ricky, what should we do? He knows everything about the human experimentation and organ procurement."

"Hal, don't panic. I'll have our people on the lookout for Sanders and his family in a few minutes. It's impossible for them to get away."

"Good," Jamison replied with an evil, twisted look on his face, "and when you find them, don't kill them. I want you to bring all of them to the white building. Sanders will have to watch while I remove the organs from his wife and child before I take his."

"Sure, whatever you like. Just stay at the house for now. I'll be there shortly."

After hanging up with Jamison, Ricky made a phone call, and within minutes a dozen men were mobilized to start searching for the Sanders family.

Next Ricky made a call that he didn't want to make, but he had no choice. It was a call to his father.

Luis was in Caracas, negotiating a business deal. He had offered to handle a shipment of two hundred kilos of cocaine. The drug would be flown to his airstrip in Mazatlan then transferred into boxes labeled as medical supplies. From there the cache would be loaded onto his boat and sail to a port in southern California whose customs agents were on his payroll.

Luis gave assurance that there would be no hitch to the transaction. He guaranteed the delivery with a deposit of gold bullion in an escrow account. It was an offer he knew his South American clients would find hard to pass up. Even though Luis didn't need the money from drugs to survive on, he enjoyed the buzz of consummating a good deal. After all, he was a businessman.

When the call came from Ricky, Luis politely excused himself from the table and walked into the hall. On hearing Ricky's news, Pedraza's face turned red, and he screamed over the receiver, "Sanders, is a dead man. You make sure of that, Riccardo, all right?"

Luis tried to calm himself for a minute before going back into the meeting room. Returning, he announced, "Gentlemen, I must apologize, but a situation has arisen back home that requires my immediate attention. I must leave now, but I'll be back in one or two days, and we can conclude our business."

Pedraza left the meeting room with his entourage trailing. They got into a limousine and sped off to the airport.

In Mazatlan, Ramon and Hector arrived at the *Clinica del Publica*. They stopped at the information desk and asked for Dr. Iberra. Responding to his page, Hugo went to the front entrance.

Ramon spoke, "Dr. Iberra, I'm sorry but we have orders to search the hospital."

"And what may I ask are you looking for?"

"Perhaps you know about them, a family of three *gringos*."

"What family? Why come here?"

"I'm sorry, doctor, but we were told to search the hospital. That's all I can say."

Iberra noticed the gun bulging from under his jacket. Without Iberra's permission, the two began walking down the central corridor toward the inner part of the hospital. Iberra shrugged, realizing there was nothing he could do to stop them. Proceeding down the hall, they looked inside each room. If the Sanders were anywhere in the hospital, they would surely find them.

Pedraza's men came to a door marked "*Personas no autorizadas prohibido*," which led to the operating rooms. Ramon started to push the door open.

Iberra spoke up, "Hold on, you cannot go in there dressed in street clothes."

Ramon held back for a moment then responded, "We have orders to check every part of this building. Don't try to stop us, or you might end up a patient here yourself." Again Ramon began to push the door open.

Hugo pleaded with them, "Gentlemen, I beg you, please. Those rooms are sterile! You need to put on special clothing before you go inside!"

Ramon acquiesced and let go of the door. He turned back toward Iberra.

"Then bring us the special clothing."

"Give me one moment." Iberra hustled over to the changing area and brought back two sets of scrubs. One of the pairs was size XXL to accommodate Hector's bulky frame.

After the two slipped on their surgical outfits, they pointed at each other and giggled like children. "Look at me," Hector called out. "Perhaps I'd make a good surgeon. I already know how to carve with a knife." Pedraza's men laughed and continued down the corridor looking into each operating room.

"They're not in here," Ramon concluded. The group left the OR area to search another section of the hospital.

Iberra, who was following close, said nothing, but inside he was fuming. This was his domain, a sanctuary dedicated to healing the sick. These two hoodlums were defiling it with their presence.

They approached a door at the far end of the hall with a sign, "*Prohibida la entrada! Vapores peligrosos: Formaldehyde.*" An insignia, with skull and crossbones, was displayed prominently just below.

"What's behind that door?" Ramon asked.

"That's the autopsy chamber. You shouldn't go in there; it might make you sick."

The two looked at each other and laughed. Ramon spoke with bravado, "Doc, I bet we've seen more blood and guts than anybody around here. Am I right, Hector?"

"I'd have to agree with you on that, *compadre.*"

The two pulled their guns out and prepared to enter the room. Iberra could tell they were sure the location held their prize. But nothing could have prepared them for what was on the other side of the door. Lying on a stainless steel table just beyond the door was a naked elderly man with the top of his skull removed by a surgical saw. His brain was sitting on a cutting board next to the corpse. The chest and abdomen were opened, and the bloated intestines were lying on another cutting board along with the liver and kidneys. The acrid smell of formaldehyde filled the room along with the odor of bowel contents. Iberra watched as the two *caballeros* suddenly became quiet. He could see their faces turn pale. Hector said, "I've got to get out of here, or I'm going to pass out." He pushed Ramon out of the way as he fumbled with the doorknob, trying to make a quick exit. Once in the hallway, Hector fell to his knees retching. Ramon followed his partner into the hallway and supported himself against a wall trying to catch his breath.

Hugo Iberra had to do everything in his power to keep from laughing realizing it could cost him his life. Instead, he reached down and helped the stricken Hector up to his feet then went over and patted Ramon on the shoulder. "Don't worry," he assured them, "you'll both be fine in a minute." Hugo led them to the locker room where he gave Hector a towel to clean up and a cup of cold water. Before the pair left, they made a request.

"Dr., please. Whatever you do, don't tell anyone about this." Ramon had a concerned look on his face as he went on. "If word gets out about our being sick like this, we will never hear the end of it."

"Don't worry," Iberra said reassuringly. "Your secret is safe with me."

What the thugs didn't know was that at the very back of the autopsy room was a storage closet in which Sarah and Josh were huddled. Josh was under the impression they were playing a game of hide and seek and that he would get a prize from his mom if they won by not being found. He stayed quiet as a mouse, while he heard the men in the adjacent room.

After bidding the two thugs goodbye and watching them walk out the front door of the hospital, Hugo returned to the autopsy room. He turned the powerful exhaust fan back on to remove the smell. Iberra took a sheet from the cabinet and covered the corpse and its organs on the table. Earlier, Sarah had led Josh into the closet, having him close his eyes to avoid seeing the corpse when they entered the room. It was all part of the game they were playing.

Hugo walked over to the storage closet door and announced, "This is Dr. Iberra. It's safe to come out now."

The door to the storage room slowly opened, and Josh peeked out. "Did we win?" Hugo Iberra gave a hearty laugh.

"Yes, Josh you certainly won!"

While his family was evading capture by Pedraza's men, Rob drove to the neighborhood where Gloria lived and parked the Land Rover a few blocks away. With him, he carried the organ bank logbook that he had risked his life to recover. Rob had the gun but prayed he wouldn't have to use it.

Once Gloria saw him standing at her front door, she quickly pulled him inside. She knew from Sarah that their lives were in danger. Gloria cared deeply for the Sanders family and loved their child, Josh, as if he was her own.

"Is Josh safe?" was the first thing Gloria asked when the door closed.

"Let's find out," Rob answered. He took his cellphone and dialed Sarah's number.

"Are you all right?" Rob asked.

"Thank God, yes. Dr. Iberra has been taking good care of us. How are you?"

"I'm fine. Right now I'm at Gloria's. She just asked about Josh."

"You can tell her Josh is well and sends her a big hug. Rob, we have a plan."

Sarah laid out how her father would be flying to the Institute airstrip to pick them up between 4 and 5 a.m. She told Rob,

"Now, all we have to do is figure a way to get us to the airfield without being caught by a city full of Pedraza's henchmen."

Rob thought and responded, "I'll stay at Gloria's until 1 a.m. Then I'll drive to the hospital, pick you and Josh up, and we'll head to the Institute airstrip together."

Dr. Iberra interjected, "Have Rob drive into the emergency-room ambulance entrance. It's enclosed so you can't see what's going on inside from the street."

Rob shared the plan with Gloria.

"I'll drive you," Gloria said. "They won't be looking for me or my car."

"No way," Rob answered. "You'll put yourself in danger."

She was silent for a moment and went on. "Luis Pedraza and his son can't be permitted to continue their evil reign in Mazatlan. I will do whatever I can to help you."

At 1 a.m., Rob crawled into the trunk of Gloria's car, and she drove to the city hospital. It was early Saturday morning, and there were still people out visiting the restaurants and bars. It was impossible to tell who might be working for Pedraza.

When Gloria reached the hospital, she pulled her car into the concealed ambulance entryway. Hugo, Sarah, and Josh were standing inside, anxiously awaiting the car's arrival. When she brought the car to a stop, Gloria got out, walked to the back of the vehicle and opened the trunk. Rob propped himself up and looked out. His eyes met those of Sarah and Josh.

Josh ran forward to hug him, even before Rob left the trunk. Then, he ran over to Gloria. Sarah kissed Rob and saw that he was limping. "Is it bad?" she asked.

"No, I'll be fine. I sutured it up over at Jamison's place before I left."

Rob took Iberra's hand and shook it. "Hugo, I can't thank you enough for all your help." The expression on Rob's face showed gratitude beyond what words could express. He knew full well that Dr. Iberra had risked his own life to save his family.

"Hugo, I have something important for you." Rob reached back into the trunk and pulled out the logbook.

"Jamison and his associates kept meticulous records of the people who they took organs from. In here is proof that my predecessor, Dr. Wes O'Brien, a surgeon from Seattle, was killed and his organs used for transplantation. His family was told by the Institute that he died in a boating accident and that his body was never found. Now we know the truth. There are undoubtedly many more names of people in here who mysteriously disappeared and had their organs taken."

Rob handed the log over to Iberra, who told him, "There's one thing I can promise you, we will see these criminals brought to justice."

Sarah hugged Dr. Iberra and said a final goodbye. She and Josh lay on the back seat of the car, while Gloria covered them with a blanket. Iberra looked down at Rob, as he took his place back in the trunk. He said to him, "Goodbye, my friend. I will pray for your family's safety and that we may see each other again."

Iberra shut the trunk, sealing Rob inside. Gloria started her car and drove out of the ambulance entry. She headed in the direction of the Institute airfield. As she drove down the street, Gloria saw a red Porsche parked ahead. Ricky Pedraza was standing inside, barking orders to a group of men gathered around. Then she saw them scatter in different directions. They were undoubtedly looking for the family she had sequestered in her car.

Twenty minutes later, they were on a desert road lit only by the car's headlights and the moon above. In the distance Gloria could see a light beacon of the airfield. *Just a little farther to go*, she thought. She remained focused on their mission. Gloria drove onward, transporting her precious cargo, a family she loved that was now being hunted by a savage gang of killers.

Through the years the airfield had seen numerous shipments of contraband come and go. In more recent times, organs taken from jailed inmates arrived there on a regular basis. Now, that same airfield offered the Sanders family their only chance for survival.

42

Luis Pedraza's jet landed at the Institute airfield. His fury was unabated, even though hours had passed on the flight back from Caracas. He was disturbed at having to leave on short notice without consummating his deal, but he also sensed the danger that an escape by Sanders posed. Luis wanted the issue to be brought to a swift end.

Pedraza was cursing with every other word that came from his mouth. His bulletproof limo was waiting at the tarmac on arrival. He called his son as soon as he got into the car. "Damn it Ricky, did you catch him yet?"

"No, not yet, but he can't get away. I have men stationed at every possible exit point from the city. They're watching all the roads, the harbor, and the airport.

"What's Jamison doing?"

"Not much of anything and it's probably better that way. He's an emotional wreck. I saw what happened to Pat, and it wasn't a pretty sight. She had a hunting arrow through the middle of her chest, pinning her to a tree. I had to take her down myself. Jamison was helpless."

Luis responded, "The real shame is that Hurley was great with handling the financials, and now she's gone. She was the real brains behind the Institute's operation. It won't be so easy to replace her."

"Father, come on, everyone is replaceable, including Pat Hurley. I'll find someone better to take her place."

"Listen to me, Ricky. Fleming has a batch of modified Chimera Factor being prepared in the bioreactors. Deals are set involving hundreds of millions of dollars. The money for the rights to the Chimera protein makes the business we do with drugs look like pocket change. This is the real payoff on the investment I made in the Institute, and it's so close at hand. I have no interest in seeing it slip away because of Sanders. Nothing must be permitted to jeopardize the success of our project with Chimera Factor. Nothing!"

Luis went on. "Jamison was stupid for hiring a surgeon who caused such problems. Anyway, without Hurley's skills, he isn't worth much. My son, you are to take charge. Get Sanders and make sure what he knows is buried with him! If he's told anyone else about us, bury them as well. You understand me, don't you?"

"Yes, father, I understand. Before long what's left of him will be in the storage tanks of the hospital's organ bank. I'll personally take his corpse out into the ocean and feed it to the sharks like I did with O'Brien."

Ricky drove around the city checking on his men and coordinating their movements. As they searched for the Sanders family, he received a call from one of his cohorts.

"We found his Land Rover in a neighborhood south of the city center. But there was no sign of him."

"Has anyone spotted the wife and child?"

"No. But security at the residential complex said the housekeeper left in her car during the early afternoon and didn't return, which was unusual since she usually stays overnight."

"Then find the housekeeper. She must be helping them. Find Gloria Ortega!"

It was 2 a.m. when Gloria's front door crashed open. Three men with guns drawn entered and quickly searched through her small home.

One of the men called Ricky on his cell to report their findings. "*Patron*, no one is here. Ortega's house is empty."

Ricky concluded the obvious. *She's got to be with them, but where the hell are they?*

He gave an order to the caller. "Find out what kind of car Ortega drives, and let everyone know about it. When you find them, I want you to bring them to me alive. Whoever finds them gets a special reward. I have to find out what Sanders may have told others. I'm sure if we have his family, he'll tell me whatever I want to know."

Gloria was driving cautiously down the dark road leading to the Institute airfield when her headlights illuminated the figure of a man standing in the middle of the road waving a red flare. She warned Sarah in the back, "Someone up ahead is flagging the car down."

Gloria stopped, opened her window and asked, "Is there some problem with the road ahead?"

"No problem," was his curt reply. "Just get out of the damn car!"

Gloria had no choice but to listen as the man pointed his gun at her. He opened the rear door and pulled up the blanket to uncover Sarah and Josh beneath.

"All right, the two of you, come on out."

Gloria, Sarah, and Josh stood in front of the car and remained silent. The headlights cast their eerie long shadows across the desert landscape. He motioned to Gloria, "Now give me those keys."

Grabbing them from Gloria's hand, he walked to the back of the car and opened the trunk.

"Ah, Sanders, you can get out now." Then chuckling, he added, "That's no place for a famous doctor!"

Rob started to climb out of the trunk when Sarah yelled, "Josh, run!" The little boy took off on his mother's command. As the man turned to look, Sarah jumped on his back screaming, "Don't you dare try to hurt my son!" The weapon fell out of his hand as he hit the ground hard with Sarah on top of him. Gloria kicked the gun away and rushed forward to help her pin him down.

Getting out of the trunk, Rob took out his own gun. "Now it's my turn," he said to the man. "Just lay perfectly still, and you won't be hurt."

Sarah and Gloria tore strips of blanket to bind his wrists and feet. Then Sarah wrapped a strip around his mouth. Together they lifted the man who had been terrorizing them only minutes before and placed him in the trunk. "Say hello to Ricky for me when you see him," Rob told him as he slammed the trunk lid shut.

"Hope he's as comfortable in there as I was," Rob said to Sarah as he rubbed his sore back.

Locked inside, Geraldo was no longer happy. Only a few minutes before, he was thinking about how to spend the reward he would receive for making the important capture. Now, in the darkness of the truck, he faced the realization that losing the reward was not his biggest problem. He thought, *I wish Sanders had killed me. Whatever Ricky Pedraza decides to do with me will be a lot worse than a quick death.*

Rob gathered his small troop beside him. "It looks like we're close to the airfield. I can see the beacon just beyond the next turn in the road. It's probably best if we walk the rest of the way, rather than take the car."

They proceeded on foot as the moon lit their path. If all went well, Sarah's father would soon be there to pick them up.

43

It was 3:45 a.m. when Randy and his friend Clay saw the lights of the Institute airfield below. They had known each other since their days as pilots in Vietnam. Although their lives after the war headed in different directions, they remained close friends. Both ended up living near Dayton, because of its proximity to Wright-Patterson Air Force Base, one of the largest Air Force complexes in the United States.

Randy had served his country well as a fighter pilot during the Vietnam War. Rather than quit the military after the war, to take a job paying a hefty salary with a commercial airline, he chose to remain in the Air Force. He was eventually stationed at the Wright-Patterson base just outside of Dayton. When he retired from the service, he became an instructor at a local flight school. There, instead of piloting jets that broke the sound barrier, he flew a small Cessna and gave lessons.

On occasion Randy still piloted jets, but they weren't warplanes. Rather, he flew business jets to their home bases after they were grounded from regular flight. Randy was one of the few men who had the experience needed to safely get a damaged jet back for necessary repair, and he was paid well for that work. Spending one day flying a jet back to its home base paid him the equivalent of several weeks work at the flight school.

After the war Clay had started his own business, Avitronix Armaments. The company did research and development on weapons systems designed for use by aircraft and helicopters. He leased a building at the airbase that served both as his center of operation and warehouse. One of his latest products was a mini-Gatling gun powered by a pneumatic compressor capable of shooting fifteen hundred to two thousand rounds a minute. The gun barrels were constructed from an aluminum-titanium alloy, which made it light enough to be used as a helicopter-based weapon.

When Randy called Clay and asked if they could take his company jet and fly to Mexico to get Sarah and her family, Clay didn't hesitate to offer his help. "Hell, yes," he said, "I've known Sarah since she was a baby, and anyone trying to harm her is going to have to contend with me first."

Randy and Clay weren't youngsters anymore, and much of their swagger had faded, but the threat posed to Randy's daughter and family got the aging warriors all fired up to do battle.

They went to Clay's warehouse at the base and rummaged through the armaments room. Taking a mini-Gatling and pneumatic grenade launcher with them, they boarded his company jet, a Citation Mustang. With Randy at the controls and Clay copiloting, they took off. There were only two of them, but they had the firepower of a small battalion. Once on the ground, they would establish a defensive position and wait for Sarah and her family to rendezvous. If everything went as planned, they would take off shortly thereafter. If they met resistance, they would deal with it.

Pedraza's men were scouring the city for the Sanders family when they heard the sound of a jet flying in the dark skies above. Ricky heard it passing overhead on its approach for landing and realized where it was heading. The landing wasn't going to be at the main airport; it was at the Institute's airfield. "Shit!" Ricky exclaimed. "That's not one of ours. Someone must be trying to help Sanders get away." He called out to one of his men, "Get hold of everyone and tell them to go to the Institute airfield, immediately!"

Within minutes of being on the ground, Randy and Clay had set up their weapons, waiting for Sarah and her family to arrive. The Gatling and the grenade launcher made them a formidable force. They were ready for anything hostile that might come their way.

Sarah called her father on his cell. "I saw you coming in for a landing. We're just outside the field, walking in on foot."

He answered, "Uncle Clay and I have your ride here ready and waiting."

Ricky's Porsche led a caravan of cars and SUVs on the road leading to the airfield. They reached Geraldo's station, but he was nowhere to be seen. A vehicle fitting the description of Gloria Ortega's was parked at the side of the road. Something wasn't right. They heard pounding coming from inside the car's trunk. "Get a crowbar," Ricky ordered.

When the trunk popped open, he saw Geraldo tied up and gagged. Ricky pulled the gag off his mouth.

"I'm sorry, Riccardo, but I didn't—" Before he could make his excuse, Ricky shot him in one of his legs. Then he shot him in the other. Geraldo screamed in pain as Ricky told two of his men, "Dump him in the desert so the vultures can have him for breakfast."

Ricky addressed the group, "Remember, we need them all alive, understand? Alive!"

He called his father, "I've located Sanders. He's at our airfield trying to fly out. We will have him shortly."

"Good," Luis said, "that makes me feel better."

Ricky's men checked their guns as they prepared to drive into the airfield, but they were certainly not prepared for what awaited them.

Randy saw the lights of the cars in the caravan go out as they began filing into the airfield. He and Clay were wearing night-vision goggles. Dawn would be breaking in a little over an hour, but it was still very dark. Sarah, Rob, Josh, and Gloria ran up to the plane. Josh greeted his grandfather with a big hug.

"Grandpa, you look so silly with those funny things on."

Randy answered his grandson, "I bet I do, but they're special glasses that let me see in the dark."

Sarah was next. "Daddy, I'm so glad to see you." She hugged her father and kissed him, fighting back tears then went over to Clay and gave him a hug as well.

"It's Clay's jet that got us here," Randy told her.

"You're the best, Uncle Clay." Sarah exclaimed.

In the distance the cars in Ricky's caravan formed a line across the runway, which would block their taking off. Sarah's father motioned for his family to hide behind an embankment at the side of the runway. He told them as they ran for cover, "And don't come back until I give you the all clear."

Through their night-vision goggles, the Air Force buddies could see men with guns getting out of the vehicles. Pedraza's voice called out from the distance, "Well, my friends, why don't you surrender to us? I promise no harm will come to you. I only want to find out some information, then you can be on your way."

Randy responded, "We came here to pick up my daughter with her family and leave peaceably. I suggest you clear the runway immediately."

For a moment there was silence, then the line of cars and men started slowly moving forward. There was two hundred yards between them when a shot rang out that went over their heads.

Clay turned to Randy and said, "That wasn't nice was it?" He went on. "Maybe we should let them know we don't appreciate that?"

"Yup, time to send a message," Randy answered.

Clay sent out a burst of fire from the mini-Gatling. At over twenty rounds a second, the bullets cut through the cars and men in its path. The sound was deafening. After less than a minute of action, the Gatling rested. One car exploded when the gas tank took a hit. Other cars scattered in different directions off the runway as drivers fled for their lives. The attackers who were on foot dropped their guns then ran away. Ricky's Porsche was riddled by bullet holes. Its windshield was shattered and the tires blown out.

Then, after a period of silence, automatic weapons fire returned. It appeared to be coming from a bulletproof SUV. Its steel-reinforced structure acted as an effective barrier to the Gatling. Clay took aim with the grenade launcher and let loose a volley of the explosive projectiles. The vehicle took a direct hit and was thrown into the air, falling back to earth at the runway's side in two smoldering pieces. A remaining SUV drove around picking up survivors. Then, it backed up, turned around, and headed out of the airfield at full speed. The quiet that followed was punctuated by the hissing of hot metal and the staccato burst from some unused ammo that went off in the flaming wreckage.

Randy called out for his family. They ran out from behind the embankment, and he herded them onboard the jet for departure. Within minutes the jet taxied down the runway for takeoff. Pedraza's gang members were nowhere in sight.

The engines roared, and the jet became airborne, leaving the smoking debris from the battle behind. Everyone onboard breathed a sigh of relief. They looked out the windows and could see the sun appearing on the horizon. Josh was in awe of his grandfather. "Gee, Grandpa, we beat them pretty good, didn't we?"

"We sure did, Josh, but we were just defending ourselves. We asked them to let us leave in peace, and they shot back at us, didn't they?"

Rob held Sarah's hand tightly. On the flight down to Mazatlan, he was filled with so many great expectations working at the most advanced transplant center in the world. Now he and his family had barely escaped alive. While the Institute had been built with the intention of doing service for mankind, its mission had become twisted through the greed of its directors. Rob was glad to be gone from there. As Rob sat back in his seat and relaxed, he found himself longing to be back in Boston.

It was less than an hour after takeoff when Sarah's father noticed an unexpected blip approaching on radar. "There's another jet, closing on us fast," he announced. After a few more minutes, the plane had pulled dangerously close to theirs. Its pilot was maneuvering his plane's wings up and down attempting to signal them. It soon became clear what was happening. The Jamison Institute emblem was on its fuselage. The Institute jet pulled up next to theirs and the pilot turned his face to them. Rob could see it was Ricky Pedraza!

Randy turned on the air-to-air communications frequency, and heard Ricky's voice.

"Please land your jet now. I'm sure we can work out a deal."

Ricky brought the left wing of his jet within feet of theirs and made some lateral swinging movements that looked like he might ram them.

"Let's be reasonable." Ricky said, pulling his jet away, awaiting a replay.

Sarah screamed, "He's crazy. He'll kill all of us!"

When there was no response to his request, Ricky came back on the channel. "I want you to start a descent and land your jet at the Tijuana airport. If you don't do as I say, I'll clip your rudder and send you spiraling into the ground."

Ricky had arranged for the warden at the Tijuana penitentiary to have his men waiting at the airport ready to pick up the passengers of the Americans' jet on landing.

Randy realized the Citation Mustang he was piloting might be able to outrun Ricky's jet, but with the weight of the passengers and weaponry on board it wasn't likely. He had to think of something else.

"Who the hell does that guy think he is?" Randy exclaimed. He looked over at Clay in the copilot's seat and said, "I'm afraid that son of a bitch has bitten off more than he can handle."

Randy issued a set of instructions to his passengers.

"Okay, listen up everybody. We're going to be fine, but you have to pay close attention to what I'm about to tell you. That includes you, Josh, all right?"

"Sure, Grandpa, I'm listening."

"Check your seat belts and make sure they're on tight. When I give the signal, I want you to take in a breath and hold it in, pressing down hard, and not exhaling until you count to three. Then keep repeating that until I tell you to stop. Josh, you think you can do that?"

"I can do it, Grandpa."

Randy went on. "This is going to be like a roller coaster ride and it's only going to last about thirty seconds, but I need you all to do what I said when I give you the go ahead. Is everybody with me on this?"

In unison, Rob, Sarah, Josh, and Gloria answered, "Yes!"

Randy called Ricky back on the air-to-air channel.

"Pedraza, maybe you think you know how to fly, but just try and get us."

Randy turned his plane down and away from Ricky's, directing the jet's nose down at a steep forty-five-degree angle to the ground. The maneuver took Pedraza completely by surprise.

"What the hell!" Ricky said, seeing the Mustang pull away. As he cursed, Pedraza followed the path of the jet's descent.

Approaching an altitude of twelve thousand feet, Randy gave the instruction to his passengers, "All right, everyone, start doing what I told you before. Take a deep breath in and bear down hard. After you count to three, let it out and take another in. Keep repeating that until I tell you to stop." Suddenly, Randy pulled out of his sharp descent, pitching the plane's nose upward at full throttle. Everyone in the plane felt himself or herself pushed deep into their seat cushions because of the extreme g-forces generated by the maneuver.

Ricky followed into the ascent. A few seconds later, he started feeling sick to his stomach. Then things got worse.

"Shit, what's happening?" To Ricky it looked like he was inside a dark tunnel that was progressively getting smaller. "I'm going blind. I can't see!"

Ricky's head spun. He vomited into his own face. Ricky wasn't sure he could maintain control of the aircraft. In desperation he slowed and tried to level off. The attempt to force the American's plane into landing at Tijuana no longer mattered. It was now his own life he was struggling to preserve.

Randy and Clay watched Ricky's jet disappear behind them. Randy slowed and leveled off his altitude. He knew exactly what had happened. He turned the forces of gravity, g-forces, against the pilot who was stalking them enough to virtually stop the flow of blood back to his brain. Any rookie in the Air Force would have known what to do—the L-1 maneuvers, which he had instructed his family to do. The repetitive straining action kept the blood pressure from dropping to low and prevented passing out.

Randy notified his passengers, "You can go back to breathing normally."

The whole episode lasted less than a minute, but that was enough to get Pedraza off their tail. The pilot and copilot gave each other a celebratory high five.

Clay commented to Randy, "That guy's an amateur. He's definitely not Air Force issue." The Sanders family was now only minutes from crossing the US border to safety.

Ricky's air-to-air communication channel came on, and this time it was Rob's voice he heard. Pedraza was still sick, and what he heard didn't make him feel any better.

"Pedraza, you're a poor excuse for a human being, let alone a doctor. I just want you to know we have the logbook from the organ bank at the Institute. It has all the proof we need to show that you killed people to get their organs. Wherever you go, and whatever you do, I don't want you to forget Wes O'Brien. He's coming back to get you!"

As Rob finished his statement, Randy turned off the transmitting channel. There was no need to hear Ricky Pedraza's voice ever again.

Pedraza was lucky to regain control of his craft and avoid crashing. When he stabilized he got on the satellite phone and called his father.

"Are they landing in Tijuana?"

"No, their plane got away."

"So, who cares? Good riddance to the troublemakers."

"Father, you don't understand. He has the organ depository logbook."

Luis was silent for a moment then responded, "Well, my son, then it appears we have more than just a little problem. We must act quickly."

Luis called his accountant and ordered him to wire his assets to a bank in Caracas. Perhaps Hal Jamison *was* Luis's friend. Yes, they had hunted and fished together, drank good wine and smoked fine cigars, but no one could be allowed to screw things up so badly and walk away unscathed. It was Jamison who brought Sanders to Mazatlan, and now Sanders had the evidence to destroy the Institute and put Pedraza in jail. Luis would have to have a private talk with his friend.

Pedraza's limo pulled into Hal Jamison's driveway. Jorge was driving. When it came to a halt, Jorge got out and opened the door for his employer.

"Shall I wait for you here, sir?" Jorge asked.

"Yes, I'll only be a moment."

Pedraza found Jamison sitting in his study, staring blankly at the painting of the Tetons hanging on the wall.

"Hal, you and I need to talk."

Luis placed his hands on Jamison's shoulders and gently pulled him to his feet.

"Come, Jorge will drive us somewhere where we can have a nice, private conversation."

Jorge drove them along a road out of town to an isolated spot near the ocean that overlooked the city. Waves crashed against the cliff's sheer wall far below. Luis and Hal got out of the car and walked together while Jorge stayed in the car.

"Hal, I know you were so close to success. But your hand-picked man, Sanders, messed everything up. To make matters worse, he took the organ logbook and that, I'm afraid, means big trouble. Hal, you may be a great surgeon, but you're not such a good judge of character. I'm sorry, old friend, but I can't allow a failure like this in my organization."

"What do you mean?" Jamison asked.

"If I protect my personal friends, like you, and let them go unpunished when they screw up, no one will ever respect me. I would never be able to manage my business. Please forgive me for what I have to do."

As he finished speaking, Luis reached into the holster under his jacket. He pointed his gun directly at Jamison and pulled the trigger. The bullet made a small hole in Hal's forehead but blew out the back of his skull. A look of utter astonishment was frozen across Jamison's face. His entire body suddenly stiffened then fell backward with a thud to the ground. Luis looked down at his dead friend, whose eyes were wide open looking up at him. A pool of blood mixed with brain matter spread like a crimson halo about his head.

"*Adios*," Luis said. "Maybe we'll hunt and fish together again in the next life, but in all honesty, I hope that's not too soon."

Pedraza turned and walked to his car. Jorge opened the door for his boss. Comfortable in the back seat, Luis took a cigar and lit it. Meanwhile, Jorge walked over to Jamison's body, dragged it by the feet to the edge of the cliff and rolled him over the edge. The strong ocean current would soon carry his body far out into the Pacific.

EPILOGUE

Rob was immersed in performing a liver transplant, but looked up when he heard commotion by the door. He gazed above his surgical magnifying lenses. Dr. Ryan stood holding the operating room door ajar and stuck his head inside to tell him something.

"Rob, when you're done, why don't you come on up to my office. You have a visitor waiting."

Before he had a chance to respond, Ryan had pulled his head out and the door slammed shut. Rob wondered, *Visitor? What visitor? I'm not expecting anyone.* He shrugged, looked back down and went on operating.

The return to work at the General was a welcome outcome for Rob. The first phone call he made after Clay's jet landed was to his ex-chief, Tom Ryan. Rob related the disturbing story of what had gone on at the Institute. When he finished, he paused then went on. "Dr. Ryan, I know you once told me never to look back on my decisions, but I have to say that going to the Jamison Institute was a huge mistake. Perhaps you'll think me out of place for asking, but is there any way I could return to work at the General?"

There was silence then Ryan answered. "Rob," he said, "this is where you learned to do the surgery that gives people a second chance at life. How could I not let you have another chance? Find a way to get back to Boston, and I'll find a way to get you back on our staff."

Once resettled, Rob found that things hadn't really changed much since he left. Most of the staff he knew was still there.

Virginia Wheeler, the surgical department secretary, couldn't have been any happier than when she saw Rob come through the door of Ryan's office to sign his new contract.

Marcus Bradford had begun his first year as junior transplant fellow and practically did cartwheels when he learned of Rob's return. Marcus couldn't wait to get in the OR with him again, so he could soak up all the experience and knowledge from his mentor.

While Rob was away, the department had obtained an important new piece of equipment. As a result of the generous donation made by Sheikh Mahafsah, Ryan had the money he needed to purchase a robotic system. Ironically, with the experience Rob gained using the device at the Jamison Institute, he immediately became the General's local expert.

Sarah began working again. Fortunately, she now had Gloria helping with Josh and would soon need her even more. A pregnancy test Sarah took confirmed what she had suspected, a new addition to the Sanders family was on the way.

Shortly after returning to Boston, Rob contacted a broker who negotiated the sale of his villa in Mazatlan. The proceeds allowed him to pay off his educational loans and place a down payment for a house in Brookline, a pleasant suburb not far from the hospital.

When Rob finished the operation he went to the locker room and changed out of the sweaty scrubs he was wearing. Sporting a fresh pair, he headed to Ryan's office.

As he walked into the department head's office, Virginia said to him, "Oh, Rob, go right in. Dr. Ryan and his guest are expecting you."

The mystery visitor rose up from his seat facing Dr. Ryan's desk and turned around. It was Hugo Iberra! He extended his hand toward Rob, but instead of taking his hand, Rob put his arms around Hugo and hugged him.

"Hugo, I can't believe it's you, here in Boston." Rob exclaimed. "I tried to reach you after escaping the Institute but no one knew where you were. What an incredible surprise."

"I trust Sarah and Josh are well."

"Yes, Josh is growing like a weed."

Rob addressed Ryan, "Tom, do you know that I owe this man my life? He saved all of us, my whole family. Without his help we never would have gotten out of Mexico alive."

Hugo Iberra said, "Rob, I appreciate your kind words, but to be honest, I came to Boston so I could personally thank you for what you did."

"I don't understand," Rob responded.

"First, it seems Hal Jamison is dead. Although his body was never found, his hospital ID, along with an empty bullet casing, were found on a cliff overlooking the ocean just outside town. DNA from bone fragments and tissue samples at the site belonged to Jamison."

Hugo went on. "After you entrusted me with the Institute's log book, I went to Mexico City and saw my cousin, a federal judge. I told him the story of what had gone on at the Institute and showed him the logbook with the names of persons who had disappeared. Within hours, marshals locked the doors to the hospital and seized the tissues in the organ bank as evidence. The wardens at Maria Madre, Tepic, and Tijuana were arrested."

"What about Ricky and his father?"

"They got away and are almost certainly somewhere in South America. Rumor has it father and son headed to Venezuela. A warrant for their arrest has been issued in Mexico and also by Interpol, the international police organization."

"The Englishman, Fleming. What happened to him?"

"He disappeared without a trace. Fleming is under indictment for illegal human experimentation and murder.

"We also found something at the Institute that shocked all of us. It seems a number of unusual animals were discovered in the research building."

"What do you mean?" Rob asked.

"Jamison used his operating room skills and the immune tolerance protein to create a number of unique animals, surgical chimeras, made up of parts from different species. Those unfortunate creatures were placed under the charge of a veterinarian who I trust. He will humanely care for them in privacy rather than see them exploited as sideshow curiosities.

"Rob, because of your courage, we in Mazatlan are now freed from the atrocities committed by Pedraza and the Institute. For this we owe you our gratitude. However, our people shouldn't have to travel abroad to get a new organ. It's high time there is a legitimate transplant program in Mexico we can be proud of. That's another reason for my visit. I came to make a request, one that I've been discussing with Dr. Ryan. Tom has offered me his support, but believes you are in the best position to help us."

"Me?" Rob questioned.

"Yes, you. With Jamison gone, the government placed the city hospital in charge of the Institute's facilities. It will soon be transformed into a regional medical center. But, Rob, with your help I could begin a new program for organ transplantation, and this time with a properly managed organ procurement protocol. Could you perhaps serve on our board and come visit us a few times a year? With your help, and the support of Dr. Ryan, I believe we can achieve great things in Mazatlan."

"Dr. Iberra, I'd be honored."

"Oh, before I forget, I brought you a special gift."

Dr. Iberra reached down behind the chair to pick up a box and placed it on the desk in front of them. Rob stepped forward and opened the lid. Inside was a pair of blue-spotted salamanders. Hugo opened his briefcase and pulled out a file of papers, placing them next to the box. "In his haste to escape," Hugo said, "Fleming left these documents behind."

Rob looked over at Hugo then back at Ryan. He reached into the box and gently picked up one of the tiny blue amphibians. He smiled at the slippery creature whose stem cells held the secret to achieving immune tolerance.

Rob thought of Hal Jamison, the man who discovered the stem-cell protein. How sad that his motives became so twisted. Now there was a way he could salvage something positive from Jamison's efforts.

His decision was made as he stood there in Ryan's office. Rob shook Hugo's hand and promised to help establish a first-class transplant program in his city.

Rob flipped through Fleming's documents. He saw they contained a formula for the amino-acid sequence of the modified Chimera protein. With all the talented people who worked at the General, he could find someone able to synthesize the immune tolerance protein. Then Rob would conduct the proper studies to establish the Chimera Factor's safety and effectiveness. Perhaps it would take a few more years of hard work to accomplish, but one day he looked forward to offering Hal Jamison's remarkable discovery as an answer for all those suffering persons whose lives could be made better by a transplant.

George Fleming walked down a bustling street in Kinshasa, the capital of the Democratic Republic of the Congo. His lifestyle wasn't bad for a fugitive. He had a new identity and a masterfully forged Canadian passport. He liquidated his account in Antigua and transferred the assets to a bank in Zurich under his new name. After fleeing Mazatlan he headed to Costa Rica. There, he underwent plastic surgery that would have made it difficult for his mother to recognize him.

Fleming, who was now known as Paul Holfield, held a job as director of clinical research for the Swiss pharmaceutical giant, Celestica. He was responsible for the design and implementation of field studies, testing the company's pipeline of new drugs on human subjects. In the small towns outside the capital where the company had its clinics there was little problem finding willing participants. Every morning a line of people formed waiting to get their blood drawn to see if they qualified for enrollment.

If they did, an initial payment was given along with a package of experimental medication.

The sun was bright, so Holfield put on his sunglasses and continued down the boulevard. He stopped at a favorite outdoor café. The waiter took his order for a cup of coffee made with rich Arabica beans that grew in the Congolese highlands. The humidity in the air made him feel sticky. It was often humid in Kinshasa, which lacked the ocean breeze of his former residence. Holfield took a sip of coffee then paused to reflect. *Perhaps the weather isn't as good as in Mazatlan, but the coffee, it's definitely better.*

Made in the USA
Lexington, KY
15 November 2014